DALMATIAN
in the DAISIES

DALMATIAN in the DAISIES

Ben M. Baglio

Illustrations by Ann Baum

SCHOLASTIC INC.

New York Toronto London Auckland Sydney
Mexico City New Delhi Hong Kong Buenos Aires

Special thanks to Ingrid Maitland

ISBN 10: 0-439-87120-4
ISBN 13: 978-0-439-87120-4

12 11 10 9 8 7 6 5   8 9 10 11 12/0

Printed in the U.S.A.   40
First Scholastic printing, March 2007

One

"Ouch!" Mandy Hope gasped. "Blackie, you're on my *foot*!"

The Labrador just wagged his tail, pinning Mandy's toes under the full weight of his front paw.

Mandy gave him a gentle shove. *"Off!"*

"Well, hurry up, then," her best friend, James Hunter, urged her. "You know how impatient he gets waiting to go for a walk."

Mandy snatched up her sneakers and her raincoat from the hook beside the door.

"He seems to know when there's a school vacation,"

1

James said, as Blackie charged out of the open door. "He can sense it's time for longer walks."

It was the start of spring break and Mandy's favorite time of year. Spring was really here. Late March had brought clear skies and warm days to encourage bright yellow flowers to unfurl and the palest green leaf buds to appear on the trees. Today, the remains of a few low, gray clouds were all that was left of the recent rain, and the sun beamed down out of a bright blue sky.

Mandy and James hurried along the sidewalk after Blackie, skirted the wooden sign reading, ANIMAL ARK VETERINARY CLINIC, and turned onto the lane leading to the center of the village. James slipped the leash from Blackie's collar and the dog bounded forward to investigate a patch of daffodils.

Just then, the Animal Ark Land Rover pulled up beside them. Mandy's dad, Dr. Adam Hope, rolled down the driver's window. "Morning, you two." He grinned. "Off for a walk to celebrate the start of spring break?"

"Actually," said James, "we're working, Dr. Adam."

"Working?" Mandy's dad looked surprised.

"Schoolwork," Mandy explained. "Ms. Summers has given us a history project to do over the break, on the roles animals have played in society. We're going to think about what to write while we're walking."

Dr. Adam nodded. "Sounds like it's right up your alley! Where are you headed?"

"We're going up to Falling Foss," Mandy replied enthusiastically. She loved visiting the beautiful waterfall that cascaded down glistening, moss-covered rocks in a narrow valley in the nearby fields.

"I'm off to help with the birth of a calf at Woodbridge Farm. I'll give you a lift, if you like." Mr. Hope offered.

"Thanks, Dad," Mandy said.

The village of Welford was getting ready for Easter. Outside the Fox and Goose, window boxes were ablaze with yellow daffodils and dark purple crocuses. In the window of the post office, which was also a general store, there were tempting displays of dark- and milk-chocolate Easter eggs. A scattering of miniature yellow chicks had been placed around the eggs, peeping out from a nest of green streamers.

Mandy's dad dropped them off on a grassy shoulder next to a dry stone wall halfway up the side of the valley, with the village spread out below. After waving good-bye to Dr. Adam, James climbed the wooden stile set in the wall, first unclipping Blackie's leash so he could shoot underneath and lead the way onto the field. Mandy followed, pausing at the top of the stile to take a deep breath of the clean, fresh-tasting air.

"So, what animal are you thinking about for your project?" James asked as they began to walk across the field.

"I've been thinking about the pit ponies used in the mines. Without their help, coal mining would have been much more difficult," Mandy said. "They hauled the coal that fueled the Industrial Revolution in the nineteenth century, and even as late as 1984, there were ponies still working in some of the bigger coal mines."

"That's a good idea," James said, watching as Blackie ambled by a pair of pigeons pecking in the stubby brush on the ground. They flapped away in panic. James turned to Mandy. "Hey! Didn't *pigeons* help during the First World War?"

"Yes, they did!" Mandy said excitedly. "They carried secret messages behind enemy lines and brought messages back on tiny pieces of paper tied to their legs."

"Those birds were incredibly smart," James agreed. "But I'd like to do something more . . . dramatic for my project. You know, something like a three-toed sloth or a Komodo dragon."

"I think we'll have to do some research on the Internet about those," Mandy suggested, giggling. "We don't seem to have many of the facts at our fingertips."

They'd come to a rocky ledge at the crest of a valley, and Mandy leaned against a gigantic boulder to catch her breath. She'd lived in Yorkshire all of her life, yet the sight of the sloping pastures neatly separated by dry stone walls, the cattle and sheep peacefully grazing among miles of heather, gave her a thrill every time she saw it. Today, there was a dash of fuzzy white and purple as the heather prepared to break into bud.

Suddenly, Mandy felt a cold, wet nose nudging her hand. She looked down and laughed. "Sorry, Blackie! Come on, James. We've got a way to go before we get to the waterfall."

They jogged down the side of the valley and began the steady climb toward the falls alongside the shallow river that tumbled between dark brown stream banks. Halfway up the valley, the river ran through a grove of tall pine trees. As they approached, the wind was blowing, and the branches of the pine trees rattled, but when the wind dropped they could clearly hear the distant hiss of falling water.

"Almost there," Mandy commented, taking off her raincoat. "Ugh, I'm hot."

They followed the damp riverside path through the trees and emerged into the bright sunshine again. Falling Foss was straight ahead of them, a foaming ribbon of water that plunged straight down the rocks at the end of the valley into a deep pool. Away from the tumbling water, the pool was very clear, and the pebbles at the bottom were colored coppery-brown. Blackie waded at the edge, cooling his paws and sniffing at the surface of the water.

Mandy picked her way carefully around the edge of the pool and found a place to sit not far from the falls, where the light spray misted her face and arms. "Magic!" she said, sighing happily. "Did you know they once used to wash sheep in waterfalls before they sheared them? The farmers thought that washing them would make new wool grow."

"Instead it probably turned their fleece orange," James commented, scooping up a handful of copper-tinged water.

Mandy looked at her watch. "We'd better get going. I told Mom we'd be back by lunchtime."

James called to Blackie as he got to his feet. The Labrador bounded out of the water and shook himself energetically right next to the rock where Mandy was sitting. She shrieked and jumped up as ice-cold droplets were scattered over her. James laughed, but Mandy noticed he quickly hopped out of the way when Blackie headed for him!

James took a couple of photos of the waterfall with his digital camera, and then they started back the way they had come, into the brief damp cool of the trees before trekking back along the open valley. The river ran more slowly here, as if the tumble over the falls had worn it out. A bulky shadow skimming over the water caught Mandy's attention. It was a bird flying low, with a black body and a white head with broad black markings across its cheeks.

"James, look!"

"Wow," James said. "What's *that*?"

"I'm not sure," Mandy said, craning her neck to follow the bird's flight. "I don't recognize it, do you? Maybe it's an eagle!"

"I think it's probably a hawk," James said. "An eagle looks like it's wearing a white hood, which doesn't match this bird's markings."

The bird had settled gracefully in a tree on the opposite bank of the river. Mandy could see a necklace of dark streaks on its throat and a small, hooked beak. Whatever it was, it was very beautiful.

Very slowly, James raised his camera and began taking pictures of the bird. With each tiny click, the bird twitched its head, as if it was ready to bolt at the first sign of danger.

Blackie had grown tired of waiting and had wandered farther along the riverbank, snuffling happily among the tangle of duckweed and wild watercress. Suddenly, he stopped short and barked. At once, the bird spread its wings and soared out of the tree, streaking upward and vanishing around a curve in the valley.

"Oh, it's gone," Mandy said, disappointed.

Blackie yapped again, a short, sharp bark that made James and Mandy pay attention. He had stopped a few feet from where a man in a dark green jacket and hip waders was standing with a fishing rod and casting over the water.

"Call your dog, please," the man instructed. "He's scaring the fish."

"Here, Blackie!" commanded James in his sternest voice. Blackie didn't take any notice so James hurried forward and attached his leash. "I'm sorry we disturbed you," he said to the fisherman, yanking at Blackie, whose tail had begun to wag in greeting.

"Nice day!" Mandy called politely.

"At least the rain's gone. No luck with the fish, though," the man replied rather gruffly. He took one hand off his fishing rod and pulled his tweed cap lower over his eyes.

"Do you know anything about birds?" Mandy asked, guessing that, if the man was a regular fisherman here, he might have seen the extraordinary bird before.

He shook his head. "No, sorry."

Mandy decided not to press him. He was obviously concentrating on his fishing, and they had disturbed him enough already.

"We can look the bird up in your dad's bird book,"

James suggested as they continued on, walking along the valley. "Or go on the Internet. I managed to get a couple of decent photographs so we should be able to identify it."

They reached the steep slope that would take them back up to the trail that led to the road. As they started to scramble up, Mandy turned to look back at the valley once more. The bird was back, perched on one of the topmost branches of the tree! Its white chin and broad feathery breast stood out clearly against the sky, and in its beak, it clasped a single twig.

"There it is!" Mandy gasped. "James, it might be building a nest!"

"That would be awesome," James agreed. "Come on, let's get home and find out exactly what it is. Besides, I'm starving!"

In the kitchen at Animal Ark, Dr. Emily Hope was slicing into a wedge of cheese when Mandy and James came in. They left Blackie in the backyard with a bowl of water.

"Phew!" Mandy said, collapsing onto a chair. "What a hike!"

"Any ideas for your project?" Mandy's mom asked.

"Some," Mandy told her, taking off her sneakers and flexing her tired toes. "But we saw an amazing bird!"

James stood up. "Can I look it up in Dr. Adam's bird book?"

"Of course," Dr. Emily replied.

James vanished for a moment and returned with a large hardcover book. He set it down on the kitchen table in front of Mandy.

She turned to the index at the back of the book. "I'm looking up hawks first," she explained. "We might see a photograph we recognize. Here we go . . . *hawks, page four thirty two.*"

"Good luck," said Dr. Emily. "I'm going to go get your father for lunch."

"OK," said Mandy, not looking up. She had found a double-page spread of dozens of different species of hawks, each one illustrated with a color photograph.

James began reading the caption underneath each picture. *"Broad winged, Cooper's, Red-shouldered, Red-tailed, Rough-legged, Sharp-shinned* — phew, what a mouthful!"

"None of these look anything like the bird we saw," Mandy pointed out, scanning the pictures carefully. "Some are a similar size, but they haven't got the same white-and-black head."

James leaned in for a closer look, just as the phone rang.

Mandy reached over and picked it up. "Hello?"

"Hello, sweetie." Dorothy Hope, Mandy's grand-mother, was getting over a cold, and she still sounded very stuffed up.

"Hi, Gran, how are you feeling?" Mandy asked.

"Much better, thank you. But I'm standing at the dining room window, and I've just seen the most extraordinary thing."

"Is it a huge black bird with a snow-white head?" Mandy asked, wondering for a moment if the mysterious bird might be circling over her grandmother's house.

"No, it's a dog! It's lying in your grandfather's daisy bed." Dorothy Hope coughed.

"*A dog*? What kind of dog?" Mandy turned to James and raised her eyebrows to indicate her conversation had taken an interesting turn.

"It's a Dalmatian," replied her grandmother. "It wasn't there a moment ago, and I don't know where it came from. Is your father there?"

"He's in surgery, Gran," Mandy said. "Are you sure it's not Elise Knight's dog, Maisie? She's deaf, remember?"

"It doesn't look like Maisie. Not from here, anyway. I haven't tried to call to it," Dorothy Hope said. "I don't want to scare it. I'm just watching it. Something's not right — I can tell by the way it's behaving."

"What do you mean, not *right*, Gran?" Mandy began to worry. "Do you think it's sick? Injured?"

James came closer to Mandy and put his ear to the phone. "What happened?" he whispered.

"Not *sick* exactly," Dorothy Hope went on. "Just tell your mom or dad as soon as you can, please. I might be wrong, but I think she's having puppies!"

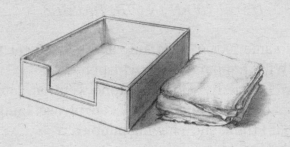

Two

"Look over there. See it?" Dorothy Hope squeezed into a corner of her living room to make room at the window for James and Mandy to join her. They were both still out of breath from the fast bike ride over to Lilac Cottage.

"Oh, poor thing," Mandy whispered. "She looks miserable."

The dog was curled in a tight little ball. Even her front paws were folded neatly underneath her, as if she were trying to make herself less noticeable. Her white coat was scattered with neat-edged black spots, and Mandy could see she had a sad, pretty face, with one large

14

black eye patch. The dog's abdomen was clearly swollen, ballooning out below her rib cage. She was lying right in the middle of Tom Hope's giant daisies, as if she'd been arranged for a window display. One yellow bloom lay across her head like an Easter bonnet.

"We shouldn't make any sudden movements or noises in case we scare her," warned Grandma Hope. "Are your parents on their way, Mandy?"

"Mom said they'd be over as soon as they can," Mandy said, her forehead pressed to the window. "One of Dad's patients needed restitching after an operation, so they couldn't leave right away." She narrowed her eyes to peer more closely at the dog. "It's not Maisie, that's for sure. I know Maisie's markings. Anyway, Maisie knows her way around the village too well to end up here looking lost and confused. And I'm sure Elise would have told us if she was expecting pups! It must be a stray."

She watched as the Dalmatian struggled to her paws and began to turn in small circles. The dog seemed uneasy, her tail tucked tightly between her legs, eyes darting nervously around the garden. She lay down, then stood up again.

"She needs our help." James sounded concerned. "She seems so nervous and uncomfortable!"

"Well, maybe that's because she's about to have her puppies," Dorothy Hope said.

"I don't think she looks very well. She might be ill as well as very pregnant," Mandy said. "James, we can't wait for Mom and Dad to get here. Let's go out to her."

"Do you think that's wise, sweetheart?" Dorothy Hope warned. "If the dog is frightened, she might be aggressive."

"Don't worry, Gran," Mandy said. "I won't get too close. But it might help to watch what's going on more closely so I can fill Mom and Dad in when they get here."

She opened the glass door to the garden and slipped out. James followed her, walking on tiptoes. The Dalmatian was lying down again but when she saw Mandy and James approaching her ears pricked up and she pushed herself to her paws. She only stayed upright for a moment before her legs crumpled and she collapsed among the daisies again. Mandy's heart flipped over with pity. This dog wasn't well at all!

"Hello there," she called softly. "You look like you're in trouble. We're here to help. We won't hurt you."

The dog stared at Mandy and James with unblinking brown eyes. Mandy saw a sprinkling of small black patches on the dog's nose. Her coat was streaked with mud, and across her nose, a scrape had left traces of blood. She whimpered once, then lowered her head onto her front paws. This was a sign to Mandy that she did not mean to be aggressive.

"Be careful," James warned as Mandy took a step closer.

Mandy crouched down, knowing that she would seem less threatening if she made herself look smaller, and put out her hand, slowly inching forward until she was just able to make contact against a warm, dry nose. "Good dog," she told the animal quietly.

"Um, Mandy," James was hardly moving his lips, "your parents are here."

Mandy didn't reply. She kept looking into the eyes of the Dalmatian, willing it to trust her and, in turn, trusting that she would not suddenly bolt away to find another hiding place. She seemed like a gentle, nervous creature, and utterly exhausted. Mandy put the palm of her hand on the dog's smooth white head. It whimpered again and briefly closed its eyes.

"Good dog, good dog. We won't hurt you."

"Is the dog injured, Mandy?" Dr. Adam said in a low voice, suddenly appearing beside her. Mandy glanced over her shoulder and saw her mom and James watching anxiously from a little way off.

"I can't tell, Dad," she replied. "She's pregnant and she seems unhappy, sort of confused. She's trembling, too."

"Hi, gorgeous," Dr. Adam said softly, bending down so that his white vet's coat flapped open and spread around him on the ground. The Dalmatian sat up with her ears flattened nervously.

Mandy smoothed the dog's silky head. "It's okay, you're safe with us," she promised.

"She's producing milk," Dr. Emily observed. "And I'm a little worried about how bruised and battered she looks. She's certainly not in a great condition to be having puppies."

The Dalmatian lay down again. She rolled over onto her side with a sigh and allowed Dr. Adam to run his hands over her. He palpated her rib cage first, feeling for breaks.

"There's a nasty graze on her chest," he reported. "And a cut under her chin, too. Poor girl."

"She's well fed," James observed. "I mean, for a stray dog. She doesn't seem to be starving."

"Oh, she's thin all right," said Dr. Adam. "She just doesn't look it because she's so close to giving birth."

"How soon, Dad?" Mandy asked.

"I'd say this brave girl is about to whelp at anytime, wouldn't you, Emily?" Mandy's father replied.

"I agree." Dr. Emily came over and knelt down to stroke the dog's flank. The dog had begun to pant and her eyes were filled with fear. "We need to get her to the clinic so that we can keep an eye on her."

"Wow," James said, furiously rubbing his glasses with the sleeve of his T-shirt. "A stray dog having puppies! That's not so good. Who will take care of them?"

"We don't know that she is a stray," Mandy pointed out. "She may have just wandered away from a good home looking for a place to have her puppies. We'll have to put up some signs around the village to find her owners."

"Good idea," James agreed.

"Meanwhile, let's get her into the back of the Land Rover and take her to Animal Ark, OK?" Dr. Adam said. "Ask your grandmother for a tidbit from the kitchen to tempt her with, Mandy."

Mandy sprinted into the house, almost colliding with Dorothy Hope, who was hovering at the door. "Goodness, Mandy!"

"Dad thinks the puppies are on the way!" Mandy told her.

Dorothy Hope looked a bit flustered. "Do you mean immediately? This minute?"

"No, Dad's driving her back to Animal Ark. We're going to try and encourage her to get into the car. Do you have some food we could give her?"

"There's a slice of ham in the fridge. Oh, poor dog!

Puppies on the way and no home to go to!" Dorothy Hope frowned in concern.

"Don't worry," Mandy said, delving into the fridge and sounding more confident than she actually felt. "We'll find her owners, I'm sure."

"I hope so," said her grandmother.

Mandy and James raced back to Animal Ark on their bikes and went to prepare a cage in the residential unit. For a change, there was no chorus of barks or meows to greet them. Only the beagle Dr. Adam had operated on earlier that morning was there, curled up on a blanket in a corner cage.

Mandy looked around, an idea forming in her mind. As Dr. Emily came through the door from the reception, Mandy turned to her. "Can't we let the Dalmatian stay in the house with us, Mom? She'll be lonely in here, and she's already frightened and confused. It'll be much nicer for her if she has our company."

"And much nicer for you two!" Dr. Emily laughed. "Sure, I think that's a good idea."

"That's settled then," said James. "What do we need to take into the house?"

"We'll need one of those really big dog baskets, filled with comfy blankets. . . ." Mandy began.

"Newspaper and old towels first, dear," Dr. Emily reminded her. "Blankets will come later, when the puppies are born and want to keep warm. And James, grab a whelping box — you know, one of the baskets with high sides to stop the puppies from jumping out too soon."

"Okay." Mandy helped James to drag the big dog basket to a corner of the sitting room under the window, where the whelping box would be bathed in a puddle of warm sunshine. Mandy found an old cushion for the dog's head.

"Here we go!" Dr. Adam gasped, striding into the room with the Dalmatian in his arms. "Easy does it. . . ." He lowered the dog into the basket and she looked up at them all with the whites of her eyes showing.

"I'll bring her some food," James offered, heading for the door.

"Just one can for now, James," said Dr. Adam. "Let's allow her to rest. When she's feeling less unsure of everything, I'll examine her and treat her wounds."

When James came back with the food, the dog struggled up and plunged her nose into the bowl. She gulped greedily at the canned meat, as if she was starving. Mandy stayed back, letting the dog eat in peace. "What should we call her, James?" she whispered. After all, if she was going to be a houseguest, she needed a name.

"Dottie?" James suggested.

"Hmm, I'm not sure about that." Mandy thought for a moment. The dog's most striking feature was certainly her gorgeous spotted coat. "I know! What about Dapple? She looks like a white dog lying in the shade of a tree."

"I like it," James agreed. "Yes, let's call her Dapple."

"Get some rest, Dapple darling," Mandy told the Dalmatian, who had finished eating and climbed back into the whelping box. Mandy bent down and ran her fingers over her dusty coat. "You're safe now. It's all going to be fine."

"There's no need to watch her all the time, Mandy," Dr. Emily said, putting her head around the door. "I think the puppies could still take a while to appear. Let's give nature a chance to take its course and leave her in peace. She's had some food and she's comfortable. We'll check on her in a while, OK?"

"OK," Mandy agreed a little reluctantly. Dapple lifted her head and watched as Mandy and James headed for the door. Then she lay down with a sigh and closed her eyes.

With Dapple peacefully asleep, Mandy and James set about designing and printing flyers to advertise the discovery of the dog.

"*Lost Dog,*" James typed.

"She's not exactly lost," Mandy corrected him. "She's

been *found*. Don't we need to say: '*Do you know this dog?*' and put a description of her on the flyer?"

"Yes, that's better," James agreed, erasing his title. He began typing once more.

Dr. Emily came in. "Dapple seems fine," she said. "I just checked on her. She's sleeping." She came over and peered at the computer screen. "That's coming along well. You'll get results, I'm sure."

"Isn't she a lovely dog, Mom?" Mandy asked.

Mandy's mom tucked a strand of Mandy's blond hair behind her ear. "Don't get too attached, OK, honey? You know we can't keep her or her puppies. Not in a busy clinic with dozens of animals coming and going all week."

"I know," Mandy said, giving her mother a wistful smile. "I'm used to that now. But while she's with us, James and I can do our very best for her, can't we?"

Dr. Emily dropped a kiss on Mandy's head. "I wouldn't expect anything less!"

James was pinning one of their flyers to the bulletin board in the post office when one of Mandy's favorite dogs, Maisie, appeared with her owner, Elise Knight. Elise was a writer who worked from her cottage in the village.

"Hi, Elise!" said Mandy. "Hello, Maisie!" She reached

over to pat the Dalmatian's head. The dog had been beautifully trained and sat down at the open door, looking as though she was smiling. Maisie was deaf but she had been trained to respond to a special whistle and she was as obliging and obedient as a dog with perfect hearing.

"Hello, you two," said Elise. She lifted her sunglasses and pushed them into her glossy dark hair. "What's this, James?" She peered over James's head at the flyer. "You found a Dalmatian?"

"Can you believe it?" Mandy said. "She just turned up in my grandmother's garden. And what's worse, she's about to have puppies!"

"Poor dog." Elise shook her head. "I hope you find her owners soon."

James finished hanging up the flyer and stood back to admire his handiwork. "We've already put a lot of these flyers up around the village, so — fingers crossed — we hope someone will recognize her before the puppies arrive."

"Sounds like thirsty work on a warm day like this." Elise smiled. "Would you like a cold drink at my place?"

"That would be wonderful, thank you," said Mandy, who welcomed a chance to spend some time with Maisie.

"I'll just buy my stamps, then we can walk home together." Elise looked at the flyer again. "I wonder how she got lost in the first place?"

When Mandy went over to the doorway, Maisie stood up and rubbed her nose affectionately against Mandy's leg. Mandy crouched down and held Maisie's head to get her attention, and received a lick on the cheek in return.

When Elise reappeared, she took Maisie's leash and they began walking across the village square toward her house. Once inside, Maisie headed straight for her water bowl, and Elise got a jug of homemade lemonade from the fridge. Mandy took some glasses out of a cupboard, leaving James standing in the hall, examining a series of black-and-white photographs of Dalmatians.

"Why is there a photograph of a fire engine here with all the ones you have of dogs?"

Elise laughed. "Look closer, James. See the Dalmatian running alongside the fire engine? The breed has been associated with fire departments for many years. They used to chase rats out of fire stations, and they also guided horse-pulled fire wagons before engines became common."

Mandy went over to stand beside James. "Really?" she said, peering at the picture. It was a black-and-white photograph, grainy because of its age. Two magnificent horses in full gallop pulled a coach on which four firemen in uniform were balanced, one of them ringing a large bell. Loping alongside the horses was a Dalmatian, panting and intent, keeping just out of the way of the flying hooves.

"Dalmatians are the most wonderful dogs," Elise continued. "They were trained to protect the fire horses from attacks by stray dogs and other animals."

"Why did they use Dalmatians rather than any other dog?" Mandy asked. "There are much fiercer dogs — like German Shepherds — that are easily trained for work."

Elise smiled. "Good question. Well, it's because the distinctive spots on their coats made it easy for the horses to distinguish the friendly Dalmatians from other dogs."

"Wow!" said James. "That's amazing."

Mandy looked at James. She gave him a little nudge of triumph.

"What?" said James.

"Don't you get it?" Mandy exclaimed. "The Dalmatian is the perfect animal for our school project!"

FOUND:
DO YOU KNOW THIS DOG?

This dog was found in the
bin of Welton lane, with
some signs of injury.
She is thin but good to
handle.
TEL: 01246 850695.

Three

At home, Mandy and James went straight in to check on Dapple, looking quietly through the half-open door so as not to disturb her. She was fast asleep with one front paw tucked over her nose.

"Her contractions have slowed down," Mandy whispered. "I'm glad she's able to get some rest. She must feel safe with us."

James nodded. "Exhausted, too, I bet."

Dapple began to make small yelping sounds in her sleep. Her eyelids trembled and her muzzle twitched. Mandy hoped she wasn't having a nightmare about her missing owners. "Somewhere out there, her heartbroken owners might be searching desperately for her."

"I hope not," James said, "but then again, I hope they are. I mean, I hate to think how worried they'd be, but Dapple's such a beautiful dog that someone must be missing her a lot."

"I know what you mean," Mandy told him, backing away from Dapple and heading into the kitchen.

Dr. Emily was hurrying around, looking a little flustered. "What a busy afternoon," she said. "It's hardly worth making a snack now, since we'll be eating dinner soon." But she still boiled the kettle and took mugs out of a cupboard. Mandy helped out by slicing up some cake and setting out some plates.

Mandy's dad had just joined them when they heard Dapple bark. Mandy shot up from the table and raced through to the living room. She discovered Dapple sitting at the window with her chin resting lightly on the sill. Her ears were pricked and she seemed to be looking intently at something outside.

"Hello there," Mandy said, and Dapple turned around. "How are you feeling?" She allowed the dog to sniff her outstretched fingers. She still seemed a little shy and unsure.

"Let's really examine her since she's awake," Dr.

Emily suggested. "I'm concerned that she's not progressing with her labor as quickly as she should be."

They all crowded into a treatment room and Dr. Adam lifted Dapple onto the table. "Look at this," he remarked, picking up each of the dog's paws in turn. "The pads of her feet are very sore."

"It looks as though she's run a long way," Mandy agreed.

Dapple allowed Dr. Adam to clean the wound under her chin and to treat the graze on her shoulder with an antiseptic ointment. He examined her all over, listening to her heart, checking her eyes and ears and the back of her throat.

"She's in pretty bad shape," he said, straightening up.

Mandy had already recognized the signs of malnutrition in Dapple. Her coat was dull and her hipbones jutted out sharply. But her dad's expression made her worried. "Is there something else wrong?" she asked.

Dr. Adam frowned. "Her pulse isn't very strong, and her heart is pumping much harder than it should be."

"She's scared!" Mandy reasoned, kissing Dapple's soft head. "Aren't you, gorgeous?"

"Maybe," said her father. But Mandy could tell he was still concerned, and she felt a small anxious knot form in the pit of her stomach.

Dr. Emily filled a small basin with warm, soapy water and asked Mandy to bathe the dog's paws, which Dapple didn't like. Her slender white tail was tucked tightly between her back legs and her eyes darted about as if she was hoping for a way to get down from the examining table as quickly as possible.

"Yikes, there's some blood in the water," James noticed. "She's *really* got sore feet."

"Sit still, girl," Mandy told her, blotting one dripping paw with a towel.

"I don't think I'll do an ultrasound," Dr. Adam decided. "Do you agree, Emily? She's so close to having her puppies that I don't want to stress her more than is necessary."

Dr. Emily nodded. "She's been through enough. The best we can do for her now is give her lots of love, good food, and a comfortable place to give birth. And, of course, try to find her owners."

"That reminds me," said Mandy, looking at James, "we've got a flyer to put up in the reception area."

"Why not do that now?" Mandy's mom suggested. "Dad and I will get Dapple settled."

"Right," said James, fishing a carefully folded flyer from his jeans pocket. "Come on, Mandy."

In the reception area, Jean Knox was muttering

angrily at her computer. Her gray hair had come loose from a bun and she was flushed with frustration. "Why on earth have you frozen *now*?"

"Hello, Jean," James and Mandy chorused.

"Hello, you two," Jean said distractedly, giving the keyboard a thump. "Oh! It's come back to life. Thank heavens."

As James pinned the flyer about Dapple to the bulletin board, the door opened and Walter Pickard came in. In his arms he held a large black-and-white cat that was meowing pitifully. "Hello, Jean," said Walter, shuffling the animal into a more comfortable position. "I think Tom's got something in his eye. It's all watery and sticky-looking. Is Dr. Adam or Dr. Emily in?"

"Both are here, Mr. Pickard," Jean assured him. "Somebody will be out to help you in a minute."

"Hello, Tom," said Mandy, going over to greet Walter's annoyed-looking cat.

"Enjoying vacation, you two?" Walter asked, gently rocking his cat. "Great weather for a school break, isn't it?"

"It is," said Mandy. "It's good to be out of classes, too."

"What's that you're putting up, James?" asked Walter.

"It's a flyer about a dog we found in the village," James explained. "We're trying to find its owner."

"Wait a minute." Walter narrowed his eyes. "You found her, you say? A Dalmatian? Quite a big dog, kind of plump?"

"Well," Mandy said defensively, "she's having puppies. Otherwise she's very thin, really. We found her in my grandparents' garden."

James looked puzzled. "Do you know the dog?"

"No," Walter Pickard confessed. "I don't, but I saw something a little suspicious a day or two ago."

"What?" Mandy urged him.

"I was on my way to the post office, I can't be certain of the time of day exactly. . . ."

"That doesn't matter," James prompted.

"As I left the house, I heard an argument down the street. Shouting, like two people having a fight. A car door slammed hard once, then again. . . ." He trailed off, frowning as he tried to remember accurately.

"And?" Mandy urged him.

"There was a yelp, which sounded to me like a dog in trouble. I looked around and sure enough, a dog was being pushed out of a car. I saw it hit the pavement, then it got up and ran off."

James's eyes were wide as saucers. "Was it a *Dalmatian*?" Mandy held her breath.

"I'm pretty sure," Walter Pickard said. "It was just a blur, but it looked spotted, black-and-white, you know. The car drove off fast. The dog looked frightened to death, poor thing. I called to it, but it ran off."

Mandy dug her fingernails into her palms. *Poor, poor Dapple.*

"So that's how Dapple got lost," James said quietly, looking at his shoes.

"Dapple?" Mr. Pickard echoed, looking confused.

"That's what we've named the dog," Mandy explained.

"Well, now, Mandy, I couldn't swear that it's the

same dog." Mr. Pickard was now struggling with his impatient cat. Mandy stroked Tom's head, trying to calm him down.

"I know," she said. She could feel anger boiling inside her. How could people be so cruel? "But it's quite a coincidence, isn't it? I mean, Dapple's paws are all cut up, she has a scrape under her chin and on her shoulder, probably from falling from the car and, after all, how many stray Dalmatians do you see in the same small village?" She stopped and took a deep breath.

"Dr. Hope will see you now, Mr. Pickard," Jean Knox called.

"You've been such a help, Walter," Mandy said hastily. "I'm sure Dapple has been abandoned and at least now we know."

Walter followed Mandy's dad into a treatment room, and Mandy turned to James. "Oh, that poor, sweet dog. Who would get rid of such a beautiful dog, right when she needs the most help?"

"Maybe her owners didn't want to be bothered with taking care of a litter of puppies," James suggested.

"But there are animal shelters that would have helped! What chance does a dog have being thrown out of a car?" Mandy fumed.

"I'll never understand people," James said, shaking his head.

"Well, one thing's for sure," Mandy went on. "From now on, we're going to make sure that Dapple is surrounded by people who appreciate her and love her and never let her down. She's going to have a great life from now on!"

Four

Dapple was turning in circles, scraping at the towels with her paws, when James and Mandy came in. She was so busy, she didn't notice she had company. Mandy watched her rearrange the bedding in her basket, pushing things around with her nose, until she had everything just as she wanted it. Then she settled into the nest she had made with a small, weary sigh.

"Comfy?" Mandy asked, coming forward. Dapple looked up warily, her body tense as though she was preparing to run. Then she saw who it was and relaxed, lowering her head and looking up at Mandy with moist, dark eyes. "Hello, girl," Mandy said. "It's only us."

James sat down beside her. He put out a hand and stroked Dapple's head. "She's so soft," he remarked.

Dapple lifted a long, elegant paw, as white as snow, with one large black circle above her slender knee, and put it in the palm of Mandy's hand. Mandy ran her fingertips over the rough, torn skin on the small pads underneath with a great sense of sadness. They sat like that, holding hands, for several minutes, until James put a curious, tentative hand on Dapple's belly and she sat up.

"How's the mom-to-be?" Dr. Emily asked, popping her head around the door.

"Did Walter Pickard tell you what he saw?" Mandy demanded, ignoring the question as her anger flared again.

"No. He was too busy having an argument with Tom, who refused to cooperate in any way when we tried to bathe his eye. He had a grass seed in it," Dr. Emily said. "Is there news about Dapple?"

"Mr. Pickard said he saw a Dalmatian being pushed out of a car on the edge of Welford," James explained. "Can you believe that?"

She sighed. "I'm afraid I can," she said. "Is Walter certain that it was Dapple?"

"No," Mandy admitted. "But it's a big coincidence, isn't it?"

"Yes, it is." Dr. Emily kneeled beside Dapple and stroked her head. "You've had a rough time, girl, haven't you?"

Dapple squeezed her eyes shut and a shiver ran through her. "Nobody's going to hurt you now," Dr. Emily promised.

"Oh, Mom, she still looks so miserable," Mandy said.

"She'll be fine," Dr. Emily told her, giving Mandy a hug. "In the meantime, I think we'd better think about dinner. James, your parents — not to mention Blackie — will be wondering where you are!"

"But we can't leave Dapple!" James protested. "What about her puppies?"

"She's obviously not in any hurry to have them yet," Dr. Emily replied. "Mandy will let you know the second something happens. Right, Mandy?"

"I will," Mandy promised. She was as reluctant to leave Dapple as James was, even for a moment.

"She needs her rest," her mother added. "Let's leave her in peace."

"OK." Mandy dropped a kiss on the Dalmatian's head. "See you later, girl."

"Bye, Dapple," said James.

Mandy's mother drew the curtain behind Dapple's basket and the room darkened. The Dalmatian sighed and laid down her head. Mandy watched her close her eyes. She wished she could take the dog for a long leisurely walk through the fields — to see her run and wag her tail. But her mother was right. Dapple was simply exhausted, and she was pretty wiped out herself. Dinner and an early bedtime didn't sound like a bad idea.

Mandy woke once during the night to check on Dapple. She found her standing up, tugging her bedding around in the basket, but as Mandy watched she flopped down again and closed her eyes. Mandy was up again early, dressed and sitting beside the dog's basket when her mother came in.

"I thought I'd find you here," Dr. Emily said. "How is she?"

"She seems rested," Mandy answered, adding, "I guess we can take down the flyers if she's been abandoned. I mean, her owners obviously don't want her, do they?"

Mrs. Hope looked solemn. "Much as I hate to agree with you, I think you're right. I'll give the local animal shelters a call again next week just in case someone has reported her missing, but I suspect Dapple is in need of a new home."

"And right now, that home is with us," Mandy said determinedly. Catching her mom's warning look, she went on, "It's all right, I know the rules about not having pets of our own, but she can stay until she's had her puppies, can't she?"

"Of course she can. Look, it's going to be another lovely day," said Dr. Emily, drawing back the curtain and causing Dapple to blink at the sudden glare of sunlight. "Why don't you take Dapple out into the yard, and I'll make pancakes for breakfast?"

"Sounds good," Mandy agreed. She called to the Dalmatian, who got up creakily and followed her slowly through the kitchen. As Dapple was exploring the lawn outside the back door, James arrived. His sweatshirt was all wrinkled, and his hair was sticking up in tufts where he had slept on it. His beloved camera was slung around his neck.

"I came as soon as I could," he announced breathlessly. "Anything happening?" He looked around and spotted Dapple behind a bush.

"Not yet," Mandy answered. "She's just having a morning sniff."

"I brought my camera," James said rather unnecessarily, since the camera was almost big enough to hide the logo on his sweatshirt. "I thought that while we're keeping an eye on Dapple, we could do some research on Dalmatians. I also want to download some of the photos I took of that big bird."

"Ok," Mandy nodded. "Mom's making pancakes for breakfast."

"Good," said James. "I came just at the right time then!"

After breakfast, Mandy took Dapple back to her basket and then joined James at the computer. He was reviewing the photographs he'd taken on the hike to Falling Foss. The screen was suddenly filled with an image of the unusual bird they'd seen.

"That's a good shot," Mandy said.

"It *is* a good picture," James said, sounding pleased. "We should make it into a screensaver for your dad. He loves birds."

"I do indeed!" said a cheery voice behind them. Dr. Adam came striding into the study, a loop of stethoscope trailing from his pocket. "I'm looking for —" Just then, he caught sight of the computer screen and stopped suddenly. "Did you photograph that bird, James?"

"Yes, I did," James said proudly.

"On our way to Falling Foss," Mandy put in.

"Good, isn't it, Dr. Adam?" James prompted.

"It's more than good," replied Dr. Adam, leaning forward to stare at the image. "It's astonishing!"

"Why?" Mandy asked. "Do you know what it is?"

"It's an *osprey*!" Dr. Adam said, smiling and shaking his head. "They're as rare as hen's teeth in England — so rare that people thought they had become extinct in the UK. Fishermen hate them because they're so good at catching fish, and a nesting pair can clear a whole stretch of river to feed their chicks." He straightened up. "I'd love to get a look at it. Could you take me to the exact spot where you saw it?"

"Right now?" Mandy asked.

Dr. Adam looked at his watch. "Well, I'm free right now." He grinned.

Mandy jumped up. "Dapple is in her basket, resting. Come on, James. Let's take Dad to do some bird-watching!"

The cloudless early morning sky had given way to misty drizzle. Dr. Adam parked the Land Rover on the shoulder of the road, beside the stile. Blackie, who had been invited along when James had raced home to tell his parents where he was going, let out a series of his happiest barks. He began to prance on the backseat and paw at the car window to get out.

"Wait!" James pleaded, fumbling with the zipper on his jacket.

James and Mandy set a brisk pace across the field to the start of the hidden valley. Mandy's dad followed, whistling. "Ah, the first primroses are coming up," he noted with satisfaction.

"They're so pretty," Mandy agreed happily, enjoying the scattering of pale little flowers poking through the long grass.

They reached the valley and scrambled down to the riverbank. There was no one around. As they approached the grove, Mandy slowed down and craned her neck upward, searching for the distinctive black-and-white shape. James pointed to a tree. "It was sitting up there," he said to Mandy's dad.

Dr. Adam pointed his powerful binoculars toward the branches, examining the tree bit by bit for signs of the osprey. "Your bird was female," he said.

"You can tell that just from looking at the branch?" Mandy asked in astonishment.

Dr. Adam grinned. "No, I spotted a ring of a darker color around her throat in James's picture. There doesn't seem to be any sign of her now. That's a shame. At this time of year, she might have had a nest in that tree."

"We can always come back another time," Mandy said. She knew how keen her father was to see the bird.

"Oh, we will," he promised. "But I'm going to notify the Society for the Protection of Birds right away. They should know that you've seen an osprey. It's a very valuable sighting!"

Mandy grinned at James, then jumped as her father gave a sudden, triumphant yell. He was pointing toward the head of the valley, and with his other hand gestured to them to keep quiet.

The osprey came wheeling out of the sky on silent outstretched wings. As she began to sink toward the stream she gave a melodious whistle, a high-pitched sound like *chewk chewk*. She dived low over the water, her claws curved toward the surface. With a flick of her wings, she dipped her claws in just deep enough to seize a plump pinkish-gray fish. Mandy could see the scales of the fish wink as it fought for freedom, its mouth opening and closing. She felt a pang of pity for it as the osprey clutched it in her talons like a precious prize.

"She's got a grayling!" Dr. Adam said. "Isn't she amazing?"

As they watched, the osprey used both feet to turn the fish head forward in midair.

"Why is she doing that?" James asked.

"To decrease the resistance of the wind. That fish is big, you know," Dr. Adam replied.

Mandy's eye was caught by a movement in the brush across the river. She turned just in time to see a large stone sailing up toward the bird. It arched through the sky, falling very short of its mark.

Mandy heard a thud as it fell back to the stony shore of the river. There was a loud exclamation of anger from behind a tree. "Dad!" she hissed. "Someone's over there, trying to scare the osprey away!"

But Dr. Adam was still looking at the osprey, his eyes pressed to his binoculars. He didn't react, except to mutter, "I can't see anyone, dear."

"Well, you're not looking!" Mandy replied. "Oh, hurry!" she pleaded with the bird. "You are not safe!"

"Magnificent!" Dr. Adam beamed, lowering his glasses as the osprey vanished in the mist. "Fabulous! What a triumph!"

Mandy peered into the bushes on the other side of the river. There was no movement now, nothing to suggest that anyone had ever been there throwing stones. Could she have imagined it?

The shrill ringing of Dr. Adam's cell phone pierced the air. He pulled the phone from his pocket and flipped it open. "Hello? Hey, Emily. Yes? Ah, I thought so. Okay, we're on our way. Thanks!"

Dr. Adam looked at Mandy with concern. "It's Dapple," he told her. "Her puppies are on the way. We'd better get back, quick."

Five

Mandy was out of the Land Rover and racing toward the house before her dad even unfastened his seat belt. James was not far behind her. She tore through the reception area and into the house at the back of the clinic. Quietly, she opened the door to the living room and peered around it. Dapple was not in her basket under the window.

"Where is she?" puzzled James.

"We're over here!" Dr. Emily's voice came from the other side of the room. She was perched on the arm of a chair, looking down behind the sofa. Dapple had a cushion between her teeth and she was tugging it energetically into the narrow gap next to the wall.

"What's she doing?" James whispered.

"She's nesting," Dr. Emily explained. "Her instincts are telling her to make sure her puppies will be warm and comfortable when they are born."

"What about the whelping box?" said Mandy.

"She's just not interested in it right now." Dr. Emily shrugged, smiling. "It really doesn't matter where she gives birth. She'll go to the place that feels right to her."

Dapple looked up at Mandy with a spark of recognition. Her eyes lingered on Mandy's face and she wagged her tail briefly before getting on with the task of preparing for her puppies.

"I'll be here," Mandy promised. "I won't leave you."

"Everything going well?" Dr. Adam asked, coming into the room.

"Not sure," Mandy's mom replied. "She seems very anxious, Adam. This might be her first litter."

Dr. Adam petted Dapple, then quickly lifted up the side of her mouth and looked at her gums. Mandy could see they were very pale, not the pinky red of a dog in the peak of health. "I'll go and scrub up," he said.

Mandy began to feel worried again. "Is everything going to be all right?" she asked her mother.

"Well, she's in a very good place," Dr. Emily said, watching as Dapple began to turn in tight circles, panting. "I'm going to get an oxygen cylinder, just in case. You two stay with her, will you?"

"Of course," James said, sinking to his knees.

Dapple came over to Mandy, who was kneeling on the carpet, and looked right into her eyes, then whined. Mandy put her arms around Dapple. She felt a shiver of fear. She'd seen lots of dogs having puppies before and she'd never known them to need oxygen. She knew her parents were being too calm, that this was like the lull before a storm. *Oh Dapple, please be okay!*

Dapple went over to the big basket and took hold of one of the towels. She pulled it across the room with her teeth, then dropped it in a heap between the sofa and the wall. She tried to make herself comfortable on it, laying her head wearily on her front paws.

Mandy and James exchanged glances. Both she and James had been present at births before now. To Mandy, the mother dogs had mostly seemed animated and bright eyed, as if they were excited about what was going to happen. But Dapple was behaving like a very old dog. She seemed sluggish, her eyes were dull; she looked exhausted before the birth had even begun.

Mandy crept closer to Dapple. "There, sweetie," she whispered. "Good, brave girl."

Dapple lifted her head and put her muzzle into Mandy's palm. Then, with one swift movement, she arched her back and her head whipped around — just as one tiny puppy slithered wetly onto the bunched-up towel.

"My gosh!" said James.

Dapple gazed at the puppy for a moment before she pulled herself around to clean it. The pup rolled around, mewling. It was pink all over, quite bald, with darker pigment coloring the skin where the spots would one day be.

"Oh, James!" Mandy said breathlessly. "Look how cute it is!"

Four tiny paws paddled madly in the air as the pup tried to roll onto its tummy. Dapple nudged it upright and, with eyes tightly closed, it began to make its way unsteadily, instinctively, toward her tummy, looking for milk. But Dapple stood up, looking rather alarmed, and moved off around the room, panting. The puppy cried piteously.

"Pick it up," James advised. "It wants to be cuddled."

"Better not," Mandy said. "Let's leave Dapple to be a mother in her own way."

"Anything happening?" Dr. Emily came in wearing her white coat and pushing a portable oxygen cylinder on a stand. "Oh! A puppy! Great. Just one?" She looked around.

"So far," Mandy told her. "Isn't it adorable?"

The puppy scrambled around blindly, crying in protest.

"Cute as a button," said Dr. Emily. "And here comes a second one."

Mandy had to get up onto her knees to see. Dapple was at the other end of the sofa, and Mandy was just in time to see another puppy tumble onto the carpet. Dapple cleaned it carefully, then picked it up very gently in her mouth and carried it back to where the other puppy lay on the towel.

"She's doing well," James observed.

"Yes, she is. It's a very strenuous thing, giving birth," Dr. Adam said. He had joined them quietly, and Mandy saw that he was wearing his surgical gloves.

Dapple allowed both puppies to suckle while she rested her head. She closed her eyes, and Mandy saw her parents exchange glances.

"She might be low in blood calcium," Dr. Emily suggested.

Dr. Adam kneeled in front of Dapple and pulled his stethoscope out of his pocket. Dapple opened her eyes wide as he listened to her heartbeat, but she didn't move.

Dr. Adam looked up. "Her heart sounds very weak," he reported, almost in a whisper.

Dr. Emily took the stethoscope and listened, too. Dr. Adam walked over to his black doctor's bag and delved into it.

"What's going on?" said Mandy, feeling the knot in her stomach grow larger.

"Are there going to be any more puppies?" James asked.

"I think so," Dr. Emily replied, moving to the side to let Dr. Adam kneel by Dapple's head again.

Dapple tried to get to her feet but she staggered and slumped back onto her towel. Another puppy was born, and this time Dapple didn't even try to clean it. She was panting very hard now, her eyes rolling.

"What's wrong?" Mandy asked, alarmed. "Mom? Dad?"

Dr. Adam looked steadily at Mandy. He reached for her hand across the Dalmatian's back and gave it a little squeeze. "I think her heart is failing, sweetheart," he said gently.

Hot tears sprang into Mandy's eyes, blinding her.

Her father went on. "Dapple is still having her puppies. Let's be as calm as we can so we don't upset her."

"Can't we do something?" Mandy begged.

"I'm going to give her a shot of amlodipine to help the blood flow more easily. And I'll give her a diuretic drug to try and shift the fluid," he explained.

Dr. Emily held Dapple's front leg as Dr. Adam clipped

away some of her coat. Gradually, he carefully injected the first shot and then another syringe full of medicine into her bloodstream. Dapple didn't even look up.

"I'm trying to give her heartbeat a helping hand," Dr. Adam said. "At least until all of the puppies have been born. After that there will be less strain on her circulation."

"Will she be OK then?" Mandy asked

"It's hard to say, honey. Her heart might be too damaged for her to recover. Our first goal must be to support her through her labor."

As Dr. Adam spoke, he turned the valve on the oxygen cylinder. Dr. Emily checked that the gas was flowing and nodded. He placed the mask gently over Dapple's muzzle.

Dapple was busy straining to have a fourth pup, and she shook her head several times to try and dislodge the mask. Mandy looked anxiously back and forth between the dog and her puppies. The newest one was almost pure white. It was the tiniest pup so far, and lay on the floor without making a sound or moving.

"Pick it up, Mandy," Dr. Emily urged. "Quick, rub it with a towel." Mandy had done this before with kittens. She had to get the circulation going and encourage the pup to breathe on its own. She sprang to the dog basket and snatched up a towel. She folded the puppy inside it and began to rub it briskly but gently. Meanwhile her dad was on his knees opening the mouths of the other puppies with a gloved finger, checking to see that their airways were clear. Dapple lifted her head, sniffing the air and whimpering slightly. As soon as Dr. Adam had established that each pup was breathing, he placed it close to Dapple's belly, where it could easily find milk.

When three puppies were in place, he came over to where Mandy was cradling the tiniest puppy in her lap. "How's it doing?"

"Okay, I think," Mandy said. The puppy was opening and closing its tiny, pink mouth, making little gasping noises.

Mandy's father checked it carefully, then set it down against Dapple's tummy. "Good work, Mandy," he said. Dapple lifted her head, regarded the newest puppy curiously, then lay down again.

"Good girl," Mandy praised her. "You have four beautiful puppies!"

The tired Dalmatian looked at her with dull eyes. *Thank you,* she seemed to be saying, *for giving me somewhere safe to have my babies.* She offered Mandy her paw, putting it carefully into Mandy's open palm. Mandy closed her fingers around Dapple's paw and held it, then bent down and kissed her head. Tears flowed down her face.

"You're a beautiful, brave girl," she told the dog.

The puppies were drinking happily now, pummeling their tiny paws against their mother's tummy, squeaking and gulping. Mandy's parents took turns holding the oxygen mask over Dapple's muzzle and checking her heartbeat with the stethoscope.

"How's her heart rate now?" James asked.

"She's very weak, poor girl," said Dr. Emily, who was listening to Dapple's chest. She looked up sharply at her husband. "Adam, her pulse is almost gone."

Mandy sat with her hands twisted in her lap. From his veterinary bag, Dr. Adam grabbed for a syringe and filled it quickly, plunging the thin needle through the rubber stopper of a small glass bottle and drawing up the liquid. Dapple didn't even seem to be aware of the needle as he injected it into her heart. "One last try . . ." he muttered between clenched teeth.

A lump sprang into Mandy's throat that made it impossible to swallow. She was about to ask if Dapple was responding to the treatment when she saw the dog heave a big, sleepy sigh and close her eyes for the last time. The medicine hadn't worked. Dapple had died.

"I'm so sorry, Dapple," Dr. Emily whispered, running her hand over the dog's smooth, spotted head.

Mandy bit her lip in an effort not to break down; James got up and walked away to a corner of the sitting room and stood with his back to them all. Dr. Adam shook his head sadly, then put an arm around Mandy.

Nobody spoke. There was nothing to be said. And then, at last, Dr. Emily began removing the puppies from their mother and handing them to Mandy. James came over to help.

"Come on," Dr. Emily urged them, "for Dapple's sake, we have to be strong. Her babies are going to need a lot of care if they're going to survive. Are you up for it?"

Mandy nodded, wiping away her tears with a free hand. James nodded, too.

"OK," said Dr. Emily, standing up. "Dad will take care of Dapple. Put those puppies in the basket then come with me. We need to find some feeding bottles and formula."

The puppies were already whimpering for more food. Mandy stood up with two of them cradled in her arms. She took a deep breath and a last look at Dapple as her father lifted the Dalmatian in his arms.

"Good-bye sweet girl," she whispered and, as tears threatened again, she quickly turned away. She would be useless if she broke down now.

"Ready?" she said to James.

His eyes were very bright behind his glasses, and wet with tears. "Ready," he said.

Dr. Adam carried Dapple's whelping basket through the reception area and set it down in the back room where the staff had their breaks. It was a bright, cheerful room that was less like a veterinary clinic and more like a living room, and Mandy thought the puppies would be happier here where they would be able to hear people without being disturbed too much.

She filled the basket with as many towels and soft blankets as she could, and sent James to rummage in her bedroom for several of her old stuffed toys. He returned with a one-eyed teddy bear and a fluffy duck.

"These okay?" he asked, tucking the toys into the basket.

"Sure," Mandy answered. "They're not exactly a perfect replacement for a mother, but they'll be OK to snuggle up to."

The biggest pup began to sniff the teddy. Mandy put the others up close to the woolly fabric of the bear. There was a moment of quiet before they began squealing for food again.

"Here we go," said Dr. Emily, coming in with a tray full of small, plastic drinking bottles and a jug of creamy formula. She set it down and began filling the bottles. "One for each of you," she said, handing them out. "I can manage two pups at a time. Of course, you two are going to have to think of some names for these adorable little guys. And we'll have to work out a duty roster, I think."

Mandy knew that her mother was trying to be practical in order to help them move on from their shock and grief. But she was struggling to find a way of coming to terms with Dapple's unexpected death. She could do no more than focus on the present, one moment at a time, and she felt she couldn't trust herself to say anything sensible or helpful. Instead, she concentrated hard on feeding one of the pups, sliding the tiny rubber tip into its mouth and tilting the bottle so that the warm milk began to flow, but not too fast. The puppy soon caught on and began to suckle hungrily.

"Oops," said James, as his puppy latched onto his finger by mistake.

"There!" Dr. Emily said, as both her puppies started drinking. "Tummies will soon be full. Are you OK, Mandy?"

"Fine," Mandy mumbled, just as someone appeared at the door. Elise Knight stood there, her face pale and her eyes wet with sympathetic tears.

"I heard the news from Jean," she began, "I'm so, so sorry. . . ."

Mandy finally burst into a torrent of tears.

Six

Elise knelt down beside Mandy and gave her a hug. James looked away as Mandy sobbed noisily against Elise's shoulder.

"Look at it this way," Elise said, pulling away from Mandy at last. "Have you thought about how privileged you are? Dapple came looking for someone to trust, someone to love and look after her puppies. And she found you."

Mandy sniffed. "We're not going to let her down, are we, James?"

"No, we won't!" James vowed. "We'll take good care of them, and find them homes."

"I wonder —" Elise began, then stopped as she caught sight of the tiny bundles of black and white snuffling around in the basket. "Oh, what a gorgeous litter."

"Wonder what?" Mandy prompted.

"I wonder if my Maisie would like having a puppy around." Elise picked up the littlest puppy, the one that was almost pure white, and held it cradled in her arms. "This one's a girl," said Elise. "Hello, little angel."

"Angel!" Mandy smiled, brightening. "What a lovely name for her."

"This is a boy," James said, holding up the puppy he'd just finished feeding. The puppy squealed in protest at having the bottle removed, opening his tiny, toothless pink mouth. "I think we should call him Tucker."

"I like it!" Elise laughed. "Mandy, is there a name you like for this one? Oh, look, another pretty little girl!"

"Patches, of course," Mandy said. The puppy had a large patch over each eye, giving her a cute, comical look. Mandy scooped her up and held her against her heart, hoping the steady beat would convey a little comfort to the motherless pup.

James got up to refill Tucker's bottle.

"And . . . another boy!" Mandy announced, as the fourth pup rolled over onto its back in the blanket. "Two boys and two girls! James, I don't think they should have more than about four ounces at a time or they'll get sick," she added.

"Tucker's starving," James said protectively, while the pup continued his plaintive crying for food. James scooped up Tucker and settled him in his lap. "There," he said. "Pay no attention to Mandy. Dinnertime!"

"What are you going to name this sturdy little guy?" asked Elise. "He looks as if he's going to grow a wonderful coat of interesting shapes."

"How about Domino?" said Mandy. "It's a very boyish kind of name, don't you think?"

"Perfect!" James agreed. "Tucker, Patches, Domino, and Angel."

Just then, Dr. Adam looked around the door. "Hello, Elise! Nice to see you. All going well in the nursery?"

"They've all eaten, Dad!" Mandy told him proudly. She knew that some newborn puppies didn't take readily to formula, but even Angel, who was the smallest and least active of the four, had quickly adjusted to the bottle.

"That's a great start," said Dr. Adam. "I've asked Simon to help out with the puppies, too."

"But we don't need him," Mandy said quickly. She knew Simon Weston, the Animal Ark veterinary nurse, would be perfectly good at feeding the pups, but she felt like she owed it to Dapple to do everything she could. "James and I can manage."

"Mandy, darling," her father said gently, "I know that you are willing, but it's very hard work looking after infant pups. And didn't you tell me you have school-work that's due?"

"It's true," James said gloomily. "We've got that project."

"All about Dalmatians," Elise reminded them. "That's going to be fun."

By now, all four puppies were curled up in a cozy lit-tle heap, their plump pink tummies rising and falling in sleep. Mandy couldn't tell where one began and the other ended. She put her fluffy duck and the teddy bear close around them, then stood up.

"Come on, James," she said. "We'd better start some serious project planning. Dad," she added, her eyes misting over again, "have you buried Dapple?"

"Yes, I have," he answered. "Under the apple tree at the far end of the yard. It's a lovely, peaceful spot, and we'll always be able to go there to remember her. This is very hard for all of us, but I know you're going to be strong. Dapple's puppies need all the help they can get — and that includes Simon's help, too."

"I know," Mandy said, wiping her eyes. "I just want to

do the best I can for Dapple. I feel like that's the only thing I can do for her now."

Her dad put his arm around her shoulders and hugged her. "You're doing just fine, dearest," he told her, kissing the top of her head. "Dapple couldn't ask for anyone better to look after her little family."

While James was logging on to the Hopes' computer to look up some more facts about Dalmatians, Mandy told him about what she had seen at the river.

"Are you sure it was a stone?" James asked, as the image of the osprey filled the screen once again.

Mandy felt a stab of worry for the bird, mixed with her sadness over Dapple. "Pretty sure."

"Well," James said grimly, "we're going to have to tell somebody if we think someone's out to harm her. Those birds are very rare in this country."

Mandy nodded. She was just wondering how they were going to fit everything in with Dapple's puppies to take care of, when the Internet sprang to life, reminding her of the task she faced right now.

"While you're looking up some more information, I'll call the fire station in Walton and ask them about Dalmatians," she said. "I'm sure they won't mind helping us."

"Good idea," James agreed. "But I've typed 'Dalmatian' into the search engine and there's more than a million sites!"

"Type 'history', too. We don't need to know about breeding standards," Mandy suggested, as she flipped through the telephone directory. "Hello?" Mandy turned her back on James and spoke into the receiver as the firehouse phone was answered. She gave her name and explained about the school project. "Yes, I'll hold. Thanks."

She explained about the project all over again to a very nice-sounding man, who introduced himself as Fireman Bob Hartley, a station officer at Walton Fire Station.

"It's nice of you to call," he said pleasantly. "Uh, you do know that we don't have any Dalmatian dogs here at the station?"

"That's OK," Mandy reassured him. "We'd just like to get some background and also get a feel of a real fire station. Would that be all right?"

"Oh, we'd be happy to tell you tales of days gone by, when firemen relied on Dalmatians for all kinds of tasks," Fireman Hartley said. "Marvelous dogs, Dalmatians."

"Yes, they are," Mandy agreed, feeling her heart squeeze up tight.

"Give me a day or two, Mandy. I'll check with the chief and find out who will be on duty that knows the most about the dogs, and when I've got it all figured out I'll call you. I'm sure we can help you make it a great project!"

He sounded so enthusiastic that, for a moment, Mandy forgot about Dapple and the osprey and the four tiny puppies who were battling to survive without their mother.

She thanked him warmly. "We'll wait to hear from you," she said. She gave Fireman Hartley her telephone number and smiled at James.

"What did he say?" he asked, as he pressed PRINT and the whirring sound of the printer began.

"He seems really happy to help us," Mandy told him. "He's going to call us back when he's found a good time for us to visit."

"Mandy, dear?" Jean Knox appeared, looking flustered. The silver chain attached to her glasses had become entangled in the top button of her cardigan. "Someone in the reception area is asking for you."

"For me?" Mandy asked, surprised.

"She said something about birds. . . ." Jean called over her shoulder, as she hurried back to her desk.

Raising her eyebrows at James, Mandy followed. She didn't recognize the woman waiting in the reception area. She wore her jeans tucked into her rain boots, and her dark hair was cut as short as a boy's. She smiled when she saw Mandy appear. "Hi, there. Are you Mandy Hope?"

"Yes," said Mandy. "And this is my friend James Hunter."

"My name's Hazel Robbins. I spoke to your father yesterday on the phone. I've worked with your parents before on some wild bird cases. He told me you'd spotted a female osprey."

James grinned. "Yes, and we have the photos to prove it."

Ms. Robbins beamed. "I'd like to see them, if you don't mind. I'm with the Walton SPB." Mandy knew that stood for the Society for the Protection of Birds, which organized regional committees to look out for rare species and protect the general welfare of birds in the area.

"You could look at them now, if you want," Mandy offered. "We have them on the computer."

Hazel Robbins nodded, thanked Jean, who was back at her desk, then followed James and Mandy through the door that led into the cottage.

Once they were at the computer, James used the mouse to bring up the pictures of the osprey. His long

lens had captured her in detail, even the purplish gloss of her wings.

Hazel Robbins gave an approving whistle. "She's an osprey, all right. Wow, this is *fabulous*." She turned to them with shining eyes. "Can you take me to her?"

James looked at his watch.

"Not today," Hazel added hastily. "I'd like to bring along someone else from the team. I'll let you know when —"

"But I'm not sure how much time we have," Mandy interrupted in alarm.

"Why?" said Ms. Robbins. "Are you going away?"

Mandy shook her head. "No, what I mean is, there seems to be someone near Falling Foss who doesn't want our osprey there."

Ms. Robbins frowned. "Are you certain?"

"Pretty much," Mandy said firmly. "I saw someone throw a rock at her."

Hazel's face darkened. "In that case, we need to get over to the site fast. It would be great for the local SPB if a nesting site were discovered in Yorkshire. The nearest site that we know of is in Scotland. And she'll be particularly vulnerable at this time of year because it's the breeding season. Look, I'll make a plan as soon as I've spoken to my colleague and get back to you, OK?"

"Sounds good," said Mandy, whose ears had pricked

up. She could hear a cacophony of squealing through the open door of the study.

"Uh-oh," James said.

"What's that?" Hazel asked, looking around. "Sounds like —"

"Puppies," Mandy finished for her. "Four orphan puppies. James and I are their surrogate parents."

"Oh, how wonderful. You must be busy." Hazel noted.

"We are." Mandy nodded, glad that Hazel didn't ask how the puppies came to be orphans. She didn't think she could talk about Dapple yet without crying. "But we have plenty of help with them so we can take you to the river as soon as you want. I think the osprey is in real danger. I'm so glad you came!"

Dapple's puppies were demanding food again, protesting as loudly as their tiny bodies would allow. They squirmed and squeaked among the folds of the blankets, clambering over the teddy bear and Mandy's duck in search of milk.

James's glasses were almost off the end of his nose, he was in such a hurry to fill up the bottles. The bottles that had to be retrieved from the cupboard at the back of the residential unit because they had forgotten to sterilize the last group.

"We'll get the hang of it soon," Mandy puffed, rolling up a sheet of dirty newspaper. "You should add more water to the formula, I think. That looks too thick."

James did as Mandy suggested, then passed her two filled bottles. She sat cross-legged with Angel in the crook of one knee and Patches in the other. Both puppies had their mouths stretched wide as they hollered for food.

"Honestly," Mandy said, smiling, "you'd think that days had gone by since they were fed, instead of an hour."

"Do we have to do this every *hour*?" James sighed, moving Tucker, who had rolled onto his back.

"Should be every three hours, from what I remember," Mandy answered. "But these puppies are just so *hungry*!"

"At least they're healthy." James put his face down to Domino, who sniffed curiously at his cheek. "They are so cute! I don't think it'll be too hard finding homes for them, do you?"

"No, I don't — and I think that if somebody turns up claiming to be Dapple's owner, we should refuse to hand over her puppies!" Mandy said heatedly. "After the way they treated that poor dog, they're not going to get a chance with one of these babies!"

"You're right about that!" James agreed.

Mandy kissed Angel, who was still sleepily sucking at

her bottle. She was slower than her brothers and sister, who had long ago gulped down the warm, creamy formula and were beginning to settle back down to sleep.

"Wouldn't it be great if Elise took a puppy?" Mandy said. "Maisie has special needs, but that doesn't mean she wouldn't enjoy the company of another Dalmatian."

"Well, she sure seemed tempted," James said. He yawned. "Is Angel finished yet?"

"Yep. Into bed, little one," Mandy said. She put the puppy into the basket. Angel wriggled until she was lying as close to Patches as she could get, her little face scrunched between her sister's front paws. Patches sneezed, then sighed and relaxed back into sleep.

"They're beautiful," James said, and Mandy smiled. He sounded just like a proud father! The puppies were peaceful and safe, but Mandy knew that their survival depended on more than the overwhelming love she felt for them. She gazed at their warm, soft little bodies. They seemed so content but they were still orphans, adrift in the world and in desperate need of loving homes.

Seven

"Mandy!" James yelled up the stairs. "Hazel Robbins is here!"

"I'm coming!" Mandy called back. Pulling on a T-shirt, she looked at the art materials spread across the floor of her bedroom — colored pencils and a glue stick — but there was no time to put them away right now. Hazel was early and James sounded impatient to get to the river.

"Coming!" she said again, speeding down the stairs so fast that her hair sprang loose from its barrette.

"Is Blackie here?" Mandy asked, snatching an apple from the bowl on the kitchen table.

"No, I left him at home," James replied. "He's not happy about it, either."

James looked as tired as Mandy felt. Their days — and some of the nights — had been completely taken up with feeding and caring for the puppies. Although they had had help from Simon and Mandy's mom and dad, Mandy could hardly remember what an uninterrupted night was like. Dutifully, James had taken his turn at nighttime feeding, bedding down in his sleeping bag on the Hopes' living room carpet with an alarm clock beside him set at three-hour intervals. But despite the fact that she was very, very sleepy, Mandy would never have missed this chance to take care of Dapple's precious babies.

"Hi, Mandy, hi, James!" Hazel Robbins called to them as they stepped out of the door. It was another bright day, breezy and blue, and Hazel was sitting in the driver's seat of a scruffy-looking jeep with an open top. "Not too early for you, is it?"

"No," said Mandy, stifling a yawn. "Not at all. Hello!"

There was a man in the passenger seat. He wore a peaked cap and had a pair of binoculars and an expensive-looking camera strung around his neck.

"Hi there," he greeted them. "My name's Steve. I'm Project Coordinator for the Walton SPB."

"Steve is great with a camera," Hazel explained, as

James and Mandy climbed into the back. "We want to get as accurate a record as possible of the osprey's visit to Falling Foss."

They set out in the direction of the falls. As the wind caught hold of her hair, Mandy hoped that the osprey would still be around. Almost a week had passed since they'd seen her with the grayling, but Hazel had been busy in her office, and their fact-finding mission to the falls had needed to be delayed. Between caring for the puppies and getting back into the school routine, now that the vacation was over, Mandy and James had precious little time for anything, let alone a long walk to the falls.

"Turn left here," Mandy told Hazel.

"How are the puppies?" Hazel asked over her shoulder.

"Getting bigger — and fatter — by the minute!" Mandy laughed. "But absolutely adorable."

"I wish I could have one," Hazel said wistfully, "but I'm out all day working. It wouldn't be fair to leave a dog alone all day."

Steve added, "Hazel told me about your orphan Dalmatians. I'd love to adopt one, too. But sadly, I'm hardly ever at home, either."

James's head was lolling by the time they reached the

parking area. Mandy tweaked his sleeve and he sat up with a start.

"We're here," she said.

"I'll lead the way, if you want," James told Steve, as the older man gathered up his various lenses. Hazel was equipped with a notebook and pen, and she carried Steve's binoculars.

Mandy filled her lungs with the clean, crisp air. Since she had taken on the role of mother dog to Dapple's puppies, her spirits had steadily lifted. Somehow, she felt connected to Dapple in a special way. The knowledge that the puppies would certainly have died if Dapple had given birth alone gave her the strength she needed to be a dedicated surrogate parent.

"What'll we do if we find someone attacking the osprey?" Mandy asked Hazel, while breathing hard in her effort to keep up with Steve, whose long legs carried him effortlessly over the tussocks of grass.

"I'll tell them exactly what the law says about protected species!" Hazel replied heatedly. "It's an offense to harm a wild bird — you're not allowed to take their eggs or tamper with their nests in any way."

But as they approached the river, it seemed deserted, with no sign of life — either human or wild.

James pointed up at the tree. "That's where we saw her both times."

"Right," Steve said. "This must be her territory, then. We'll settle down to keep watch somewhere where we won't be noticed so we don't scare her off. How about behind that bush over there?"

Mandy was pleased to sit down. She leaned against a smooth rock and stretched out her legs, feeling the warm sunbaked stone through her sweatshirt. James asked Steve endless technical questions about photography, until Mandy began to feel her eyelids closing. A couple of yards away, Hazel sat still as a statue and scanned the sky for signs of the osprey. She was so patient! An hour passed, then two. Mandy spotted a vole scurrying in the undergrowth, tracked the busy progress of a colony of ants, and gave in to her heavy eyelids and dozed a bit. It was deathly quiet, and then her tummy rumbled loudly. All she'd had was an apple for breakfast.

"Seems we're not going to be lucky, after all," Hazel said at last, taking the binoculars from around her neck.

Mandy yawned and stretched, gazing up into the blue dome above her head. "What's that?" she said suddenly. "Look!"

A pinpoint of dark movement was heading arrow-fast

toward the water. A heartbeat later, the osprey appeared, her mighty wings beating powerfully. Catching a thermal gust, she glided as lightly as a feather, weaved through the trees, and was gone.

"Fantastic!" said Steve.

Hazel scrambled to her feet. "Let's see if we can find a nest."

Mandy jumped up, wide awake now. The osprey was still here!

Steve led the way across the river by hopping from rock to rock. On the opposite bank, the densely growing trees cast them into cool, damp shade. Hazel kept an eye on the topmost branches, and James did the same, almost walking into a trunk in his path.

Mandy craned her neck, shading her eyes against the brightness of the sky. And, suddenly, there it was — a round cluster of twigs resting in the crook between two sturdy branches.

"There!" she cried, pointing. The messy-looking nest was carefully balanced as close to the top of the tree as it could be, and Mandy wondered aloud how they were going to reach it.

"It's not impossibly high," Hazel commented. "Ospreys have been known to build their nests more than two hundred feet off the ground."

"This one's nothing like that," Steve added. "I'd like to check to see if there are any eggs in the nest. Who'd like to come with me?"

"I'll go!" Mandy said quickly, thrilled but nervous.

"Great," he said, handing his camera to James. "I'll go first."

"What if the osprey comes back now?" James asked, checking for the bird. "She might feel threatened."

"We're not going to be here very long," Hazel replied as she began to unload the contents of her backpack. "Here, Mandy, let me help you with your kit."

"Kit?" said Mandy.

"Just in case you slip while you're climbing," Hazel explained. She unpacked a coil of nylon rope and a pulley. She fastened a stiff fabric belt around Mandy's waist and adjusted it so that it fit snugly. Steve was putting on his own belt.

"You look like you're going to climb a mountain!" James observed.

"The equipment's very similar," Steve agreed. He threw the end of the rope over the nearest branch and hauled himself up.

Hazel had attached Mandy's belt to Steve's so that they were roped together.

"I'm an experienced climber," he told Mandy, grinning

down at her from his perch up on the branch. "If you lose your footing, I can carry your weight and lower you safely to the ground, OK?"

"Up you go, Mandy," said Hazel.

It wasn't a hard tree to climb, but the nest still seemed a very long way up when Mandy pulled herself onto the lowest branch. Luckily, the soles of her sneakers clung without difficulty to the evenly spaced branches, and there were plenty of places to grip with her hands. Steve was soon far above her, until it became too difficult for him to go on and he sat hunched among the leaves in a tangle of tight branches.

"You're smaller than me," he said as Mandy climbed up to join him. "Can you keep going? I'll be here. You'll be very safe."

Mandy nodded, too winded to speak. On she went, higher and higher, and with each branch she felt her heart beat a little faster. Once, she felt the tug of the rope at her waist and looked back down at Steve, who was playing out the rope to give it more slack.

"Good job," he said. "You're almost there. Keep going."

She continued on, not daring to look down anymore. At last she hooked her right hand over the branch nearest the nest and hauled herself up until her head was level with the osprey's home. Close up, it wasn't just a clumsy collection of sticks, there were patches of cow manure woven in among the twigs to hold them together, plus a couple of pieces of trash — a scrap of a cardboard carton and a piece of cloth. Mandy hoisted herself into a sitting position, straddling a long, thin branch, and peered into the nest.

"Eggs!" she cried. "There are three eggs in the nest! They're kind of pink, with brownish and dark green markings."

"That's great!" Steve called back. "Those are defi-

nitely osprey eggs. Come down now, Mandy. But be careful, OK?"

He watched Mandy descend slowly, until she passed him in the tree, then he, too, began to climb down. Mandy looked down to see Hazel and James jumping around below in a little dance of excitement.

"This is fantastic news!" Steve said enthusiastically, as he arrived on the ground behind Mandy. She was flushed and hot and triumphant, and Hazel gave her a hug.

"We're going to have to set up a blind as soon as we can to watch the chicks," Hazel said. "That's a green-colored tent from where we can watch without being seen by the ospreys," she added when James looked puzzled. "Let's get back to Walton and set up a rotation of people to observe."

"We'll help," Mandy offered at once. "The puppies are growing up. They need to be fed fewer times at night now, and Simon won't mind doing an extra feeding or two when he hears about the nest."

"We'll work it out," Hazel said happily. "Thank you, both of you. Now, let's get home and start making plans!"

Back at Animal Ark, James and Mandy headed straight for the puppies. They found Simon spread out on the floor beside them with his head propped in his hand.

Patches had hold of his belt buckle, Domino his shoe lace, while Tucker was tugging on his earlobe. Angel was curled up as close to Simon as she could get, sucking on his little finger. "Hi there." He grinned. "Have you come to relieve me?"

"If you want us to," Mandy said.

She and James squeezed in beside Simon and gathered the puppies to them for hugs and kisses of greeting. They were just able to wag their tails now, happily acknowledging the two people they knew and loved best in the world. Angel, particularly, had become attached to Mandy and now she ambled over for a cuddle, her tiny tail waving from side to side. Mandy kissed her nose.

"So," Simon asked, easing out of his cramped position, "did you see the osprey?"

"We did!" James punched the air in triumph. "And we found the nest."

"Really?" Simon looked impressed.

"Three eggs, too," Mandy reported. "We were so lucky."

"You'll have to watch it," Simon warned. "Those eggs are extremely valuable and if news gets out, thieves could start taking an interest."

"We know," James said gloomily. "And fishermen

hate the birds because they're better at catching fish than people are."

There was a tapping on the door behind them. Simon opened it for Elise, who had Maisie with her on a leash.

"Hello, Simon," she said.

"Hi, Elise." He smiled, as he edged aside to let her pass into the room. "There's not much room in here so I'll get back to work and leave you with them."

"Bye, Simon — and thanks!" Mandy called, then she greeted Elise and Maisie.

"I checked with your mom, Mandy," said Elise. "She said it would be all right to introduce Maisie to the puppies because Maisie has had all of her shots."

"Oh, yes," Mandy agreed. "We're sure Maisie is safe. Come and sit here."

Maisie stood stock-still. She seemed nervous and surprised by the scent of the small bundles on the floor. She tried to back out of the room but Elise encouraged her to lie down beside her chair. She obeyed but her eyes darted around. Mandy watched anxiously. She was hopeful that Maisie would be relaxed and happy around the puppies, so that Elise would feel confident about adopting one of them. But she knew that Elise hadn't made up her mind yet — which meant that the outcome of this visit by Maisie would be critical.

"Oh, dear," Elise said. "She doesn't seem happy to meet them, does she?"

Mandy stood up with Angel in her arms. She walked over and gently put the puppy in Elise's lap. Angel lay there, making little snuffling noises as she sensed Maisie's presence. Maisie looked at the pup in her owner's lap, then looked away.

"Maisie, darling," Elise said. "It's OK. . . ."

Then Angel began to whimper. She was looking for Mandy; she didn't recognize Elise's scent and she felt too far off the ground to be safe. Angel gave a small whine of distress — and although Maisie couldn't hear, she seemed to react instinctively to Angel's anxiety. She stood up and came around to where the puppy lay. She licked her with her long, warm tongue over and over until the puppy lay still, blinking up with round blue eyes at the big dog.

"Maisie has a mother's instincts!" Elise said softly.

Mandy nodded. "She's so gentle."

"Good girl, Maisie," said James, who was changing away the soiled newspapers under Domino. "I'll get some clean paper," he added and began rolling up the old paper.

"So, Maisie," Elise murmured, stroking her dog's smooth head. "Do you like the puppy?"

Maisie wagged her tail, looking up at Elise with her trusting brown eyes.

Elise smiled. "I think that's a yes!" She looked at Mandy. "Well, I love Angel, too, and I'd love to give her a home, Mandy, if that's all right with you."

Mandy sprang up and hugged her. "It's more than all right! It's amazing and fantastic. I'm so happy — for you and for Maisie — but especially for Angel!"

Eight

"Pass the stapler, please," said James.

Mandy reached across Domino and Tucker, who were wrestling on her knees, and received a thorough face washing from loving little tongues as she bent down. She handed the stapler to James and concentrated on unhooking Domino's tiny claws from the sleeve of her sweater.

Dapple's puppies had recently been weaned on to solid food, and Tucker's face was smeared with puppy food. Some of it had gotten into Mandy's hair, and she used her free hand to pick it out.

Dr. Emily put her head around the door. "Doing the project while puppy-sitting?" she asked when she saw the printouts and materials spread out on the floor. "That's ambitious." She sat down on the floor, and Patches scuttled over to greet her. The puppy stood up on her hind legs to take hold of the long, auburn pony-tail hanging down Dr. Emily's back and gave it a tug.

"James!" Mandy wailed, pointing to a page that had floated onto the floor. Domino had pounced on it and left a puppy-food-colored paw print on the paper.

"Yikes," said James, snatching it up. "Maybe this isn't such a good idea."

Domino trotted over to Mandy and began chewing her sneaker laces.

"You're such a little live wire," she told him. "Why can't you keep still like your sister?"

Angel was in Mandy's lap, as usual. She liked it even better when Mandy was lying down so that she could clamber onto her chest and lie where she could feel the beating of Mandy's heart. At four weeks, the puppies were beginning to be adventurous — Patches particularly. She was the one who scratched the door with her tiny front paw, looking around at James or Mandy as if to say, "Can I go out and explore now?"

"What are you two up to today?" Dr. Emily said.

"Hazel Robbins is coming to pick us up pretty soon," said James. "We're going to Falling Foss to help build a blind!"

"And Dad's giving us a lift to the Walton fire station later this afternoon for our interview," Mandy added.

"It's going to be a busy day," her mom commented.

Mandy carried Angel back to the basket, and she snuggled into the folds of a blanket. Then Mandy began gathering up the food bowls to wash them. James was rolling a Ping-Pong ball for Tucker and Domino to chase. They hurried after it, colliding with each other as the ball rounded the leg of a chair. Tucker squeaked and fell down.

"Oops!" James said, scooping up the puppy and holding him close. "Crash landing! Are you OK?"

"He's fine," Dr. Emily said, as Tucker shook his head. "All part of the learning experience."

"Mandy?" Dr. Adam opened the door. "I just got a call from a friend of Grandpa's. Do you remember Phillip Hearn? He had a Springer spaniel named Bonnie."

Mandy smiled. "Oh, yeah, I remember Bonnie."

"Unfortunately, Bonnie had to be put to sleep six months ago," Dr. Adam went on. "But Mr. Hearn heard about Dapple's litter and he's very eager to give a puppy a home."

"He's always had dogs," Dr. Emily added. "He'd be able to provide a great home."

"That's fantastic!" Mandy said. "Which one does he want? I mean, boy or girl?"

"He asked for a female," Dr. Adam replied.

Just then, there was a honk from a car horn from outside.

"That's Hazel," Mandy said. "Ready, James?"

"Ready!" said James.

"Have a great time!" called Dr. Emily. She bent down to grab Patches as Mandy opened the door.

"Sorry, little one," said Mandy. "You can't come with us today. Bye, Mom. Bye, Dad! We're off to save some ospreys!"

Outside, Hazel Robbins was clearing some room for James and Mandy to sit among a stack of magazines on the backseat of the car. Steve was there, and another man they hadn't met. Hazel did the introductions.

"Nice to meet you," said the man, whose name was Stuart. "We really appreciate you giving up your weekend to help out."

"No problem," said James, climbing into the back. He pulled a canvas bag bulging with equipment onto his lap to make space for Mandy.

"We love birds," Mandy added. "And it's such an honor that the ospreys have come to nest in Welford!"

"That's how *we* feel! Are you all buckled up?" Hazel glanced around to check on her passengers, then started the engine.

Once they had reached the shoulder of the road by the stile, they passed out the supplies. Mandy carried a load of light aluminum poles with which they would secure the canvas hide. James held a plastic crate containing binoculars, notebooks, clipboards, and one small, foldable footstool. Between them, Stuart and Steve carried the folded blind itself, while Hazel volunteered to transport ropes, pulleys, and the rest of the climbing equipment packed into the unwieldy-looking bag that had been on James's knees.

As they made their way down into the hidden valley, James said quietly, "Any fishermen lurking around?"

"Can't see anyone," Mandy replied, relieved, and shifted her poles to the other hip.

Steve and Stuart located a site for the blind halfway up the valley, on the opposite side from the osprey's nest.

"This should be the perfect spot," said Hazel, easing the bag to the ground. "We're close enough to train our binoculars on the ospreys but far enough away not to alarm them."

"How do we start?" Mandy was eager to begin.

"Thread the poles through the base of the fabric," Hazel instructed, pointing as the blind was unrolled. "Then hook the ends into the brass grommets on each corner. Like this."

Mandy soon got the hang of it and in no time the dome of the blind was taking shape. The green-and-brown dappled outer covering was the perfect camouflage against the grass and bracken lining the valley.

James unrolled the ropes attached to each corner of the tent and began to peg them into the ground. Mandy then focused on the windows, following Hazel's instructions to tie up the material flaps on the front opening, which faced the nest. Supplies were loaded into the blind, and Mandy set up the stool at the window where Stuart was positioning his camera.

"Can I look?" James asked.

Stuart nodded, and edged out of the blind to let James crawl in. It was only about six feet square at the base and it was a bit of a squash with all of them in there, but Mandy didn't mind.

After fifteen minutes her legs began to get pins and needles and there had been no sign of the ospreys. She wriggled as quietly as she could, until James dug her in the ribs. "You're sitting on my toes," he complained.

"Sorry!" Mandy whispered. She decided the best plan

was to kneel up, which brought her eyes level with the camera fixed in the side window. She peered through the long lens and gasped. "Wow! There are *two* ospreys above the nest!"

A hush fell over the blind as everyone turned to look. Mandy kept her eyes glued to the camera. The female bird was circling the nest with another osprey that Mandy guessed was her mate. Suddenly, the female bird folded her wings and dived down into the trees.

Mandy watched the male bird land carefully on the edge of the nest, peering in to keep watch over the clutch of eggs.

There was a chorus of delighted chatter from outside the hut, and Mandy tore herself away from Steve's camera to join in the excitement.

"Fantastic!" Stuart and Steve were saying. "What a great sighting!"

"What happens next?" Mandy asked.

"We'll take turns watching," Steve said. "You too, if you want to. We can't man the blind twenty-four hours a day, unfortunately, but we'll do our best to be here during daylight hours."

Mandy and James stayed for another hour, sometimes sitting inside the hide at the windows and sometimes lying very quietly in the bracken to watch the birds circle above the fragile treetop nest. Suddenly,

Mandy realized they would have to head home if they wanted enough time to get ready for the appointment at the fire station. "We have to get back pretty soon," she told Hazel. "Is that OK?"

"Sure," Steve said. "We'll take you. And thanks, both of you, for your help today. You've played a big part in keeping these birds safe, and you should feel very proud of yourselves!"

Mandy and James took the bus into Walton, which dropped them at the town center. From there, it was a short walk to the fire station. Mandy stopped at the door to tuck her T-shirt into her jeans and brush her hair. It had been a rush getting ready, but they were confident leaving the puppies with Simon, who had promised to give them their third meal of the day.

James rapped on the open door of a small office. A friendly looking man with curly brown hair was sitting at a table, drinking a mug of tea. He looked up and smiled. "Come in!"

"Hello," said Mandy. "I'm Mandy Hope and this is my friend James Hunter. We called about talking to someone who could help us with a school project."

"I remember. I'm Fireman Hartley. You spoke to me," he said, standing up and coming over to greet them. After they had shaken hands, he said, "Would you like

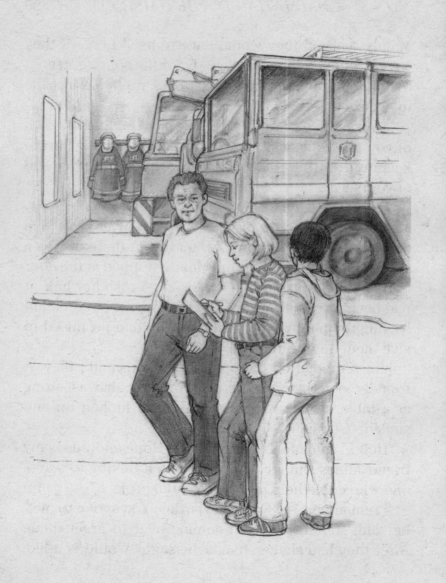

to look around first? It might help to get a feel of what a modern fire station is like, so you can compare it with how things were a hundred years ago."

Mandy nodded. "That would be great, thanks."

They followed Fireman Hartley through a door at the back of the office. Mandy had her notebook ready as they stepped into a huge room with a smooth concrete floor. Three gleaming-red fire engines were parked in front of folding doors that led on to the driveway. A row of yellow helmets hung on hooks along the wall, with a thick maroon coat underneath each one.

"I'll start by showing you the nerve center of the operation," said Fireman Hartley, opening another door. "This is the dispatch room."

A man and a woman in casual clothes sat at desks facing each other, with computers in front of them. On a table at the side of the room, two printers were churning out reams of paper.

"Give me your precise location, please," said the woman, speaking into the headset telephone she was wearing.

"These two are part of the part-time crew," Fireman Hartley explained. "About half the squad are permanent, and the rest are part-time, which means they have other jobs but help out in an emergency."

"I love the pictures of the Dalmatians," Mandy said. Her attention had been caught by a series of sepia-toned photographs on the wall above the printers. They looked like the one in Elise Knight's cottage, except in these pictures the Dalmatians running alongside the engines wore small jackets with Walton Fire Service emblazoned across their backs.

Fireman Hartley smiled. "They're such an important part of the history of fire departments, but people rarely hear about them now. They were chosen as fire dogs because they are very physical dogs, strong, muscular, and easily trained, too. They can run alongside a horse and keep up for as many as twenty or thirty miles a day."

He led them up a flight of stairs to the recreation room. There was a pool table and a television set on one side and a small kitchen on the other. A member of the crew was draining a colander of spaghetti.

"Hi, there," he said, smiling at James and Mandy. "Hi, Bob."

"That looks good, Jeff," said Fireman Hartley, nodding toward the pasta. "Save some of that for me, OK?"

"Another Dalmatian!" Mandy said, pointing to a framed photograph standing on a shelf. In this one, the dog sat on the driver's seat of an engine, the arm of a grubby-looking fireman slung around the dog's shoulders.

Fireman Hartley grinned. "That's Minnie. She lived to be nearly seventeen years old. When fire engines were horse drawn, almost every fire station in England had a Dalmatian to keep the horses company and guard the firehouse. They're very protective, loyal dogs."

"Do you have one here?" James asked, looking around. "A Dalmatian, I mean?"

Bob Hartley shook his head. "Modern fire stations don't need Dalmatians, thanks to technological advances in our equipment. The end of the era for Dalmatians came when fire engines were motorized, when the dogs could no longer keep up on the way to putting out fires."

"We're taking care of a litter of Dalmatian puppies," James told him.

"Really?" Fireman Hartley looked interested.

"The mother dog died," Mandy explained. "James and I are in charge of the puppies until they find new homes."

"That's sad," he said. "Are the puppies doing well?"

"Very well!" said Mandy. "They're wonderful."

They followed Fireman Hartley into a room lined with metal racks containing breathing apparatuses, fire suits, and masks. In one corner, Mandy noticed a shiny metal pole leading down through a large round hole in the floor.

"Careful." Fireman Hartley put out a warning hand and halted James midstride. "Don't fall down the hole! Apparently, long ago, fire stations had regular stairs until the horses down below learned how to climb them and came up looking for food!"

Mandy laughed.

Now that they had seen all the rooms in the fire station, Fireman Hartley led them outside to a small, pretty garden. A wooden bench sat at the edge of a tiny square of lawn, edged with tulips and daffodils.

"Take a seat," invited Bob Hartley.

"What a beautiful garden," said Mandy, sitting beside him.

"The crew takes good care of it. It's a great place to eat lunch," he said.

Stretching out her legs in the sunshine, Mandy noticed a little rectangular stone encircled by ferns. It had been engraved, but she couldn't see what was written on it.

Fireman Hartley followed her gaze. "That's a memorial to Ebb and Flow, a pair of Dalmatians owned by the Walton fire station in the early 1900s," he said. "They became famous after a fire broke out in the local hospital.

The dogs ran all the way to the hospital, keeping up with the team of horses, then comforted the patients when they had been led to safety."

"We'll definitely include them in our project," said Mandy. "Thanks for all your help, Fireman Hartley."

"It's been fun!" he said, standing up. "My daughter goes to Walton School, too, so I know how important it is to get these projects right. But I'd better be getting back to work." He walked with them to the front of the fire station. "Come back anytime," he invited.

"We'll send you a copy of our project when it's finished," Mandy offered.

"I'd like that!" he said.

James waved, and the two friends set off for the bus stop.

"I think we've got plenty for the project now, don't you?" Mandy said.

"Oh, yeah," James said. "But I'm sad that Walton's fire station doesn't have its own Dalmatian anymore. It should."

Mandy stopped walking, even though she could see a bus heading toward their stop. "James," she said. "Do you think we could persuade Fireman Hartley to take Tucker and Domino?"

James nodded enthusiastically "He'd be a great owner! And Walton Fire Station would have a pair of pups once more." Mandy grinned. "We'll have to get back in touch with him and make a case for the puppies as soon as we can."

Back at Animal Ark they discovered the puppies tumbling around energetically. Mandy surveyed the chaos in their little room. "Uh-oh," she said, turning to make a face at James. "It's playtime!"

James stepped into the room behind her. "Teddy's lost a front paw," he observed, holding the plush bear up to examine.

"Poor Teddy," said Mandy, frozen to the spot to avoid stepping on the puppies.

Tucker began making little yipping noises, and James picked him up. "Tucker is very noisy," he said. "He always makes his opinions well known. Should I get some fresh newspaper?"

"OK," Mandy answered, bending down to pet Angel. She had just sat down to give the puppies her full attention when James came bursting back into the room. He was carrying an armful of discarded newspapers and looked very angry.

"Look at this!" he said, thrusting the latest copy of the *Walton Gazette* under Mandy's nose.

"What?" Mandy took the paper and read the letters page where James was pointing.

James couldn't keep quiet. "How can they do this? There's a letter from a group of local fishermen who are protesting about the ospreys' nest being *protected* by the SPB!" he said, sounding as if he were about to explode.

"'*Ospreys have been known to clear the fish from whole stretches of a river,*'" Mandy read aloud. "'*As residents who have paid for licenses to fish these waters, we demand to be able to fish without being policed; we demand our share of the fish these birds are taking from our river. As Falling Foss is a popular tourist attraction, it would surely be in the best interests of the birds to be relocated to a remote area where they will have a better chance of not being disturbed by those who wish to enjoy our river — and safer from thieves who could be after their eggs.*'"

Mandy threw down the newspaper, and Angel promptly sat on it and began chewing a corner. "They're exaggerating!" she cried. "There's only one nest. How many fish can one pair of ospreys eat?"

"But if the chicks hatch, there'll be more ospreys, won't there?" James pointed out. "Do you want to go down to the falls today? Blackie's dying for a good run. Plus, I lost a penlight I had in my pocket when we went to help with the blind. We could look for it and check on the nest at the same time."

Mandy glanced down at the floor and saw that all four puppies were climbing into their basket for a nap. The fire-dog project was coming along well — and the sun was shining temptingly through the window above the sink.

"Go get Blackie — let's go!"

Simon Weston offered them a lift to a field near the falls. It was his afternoon off and he had arranged to meet some friends in Walton.

"Thanks, Simon," Mandy said, climbing into the front of the car as James secured Blackie in the rear of Simon's roomy sedan.

"Your dad showed me James's photo of the osprey. It's magnificent! I wish I had time to come with you to the blind," he said, as he carefully turned down the narrow lanes out of Welford. Mandy pointed out the grassy shoulder by the stile, and he slowed to a stop.

"Here?"

"Yup," James told him, hopping out. "It's an easy walk from here to the river. Thanks."

"Bring back more pictures!" Simon called as he drove away.

They climbed over the stile and onto the field, where James let Blackie run free. He tore off, giving a volley of happy barks, his tail wagging hard.

They walked swiftly, remembering that it was already late afternoon, and they needed to get back before dark. James kept an eye out for his penlight, and Mandy watched for signs of fishermen. She was out of breath when they reached the river, which, after the recent rainfall, was racing along in full speed.

"No sign of it!" James said gloomily, his eyes on the ground. "It was a Christmas present, too."

"Don't give up," Mandy said. "We might still find it."

Blackie drank deeply from the river, then began to scrape at a big, loose stone with his front paw. Mandy sat down on the bank and gazed upward, scanning the sky. "Please," she begged the birds, "please be here. Please be OK!"

As though in answer, there was a stuttering cry and an osprey appeared above the trees.

Mandy gasped. "James, look, it's carrying something — and it's not a fish!"

James shaded his eyes from the glare of the sun. "It looks like a vole or a small rat."

The osprey swooped above them in a wide circle, then folded its wings and sank neatly into the tree where James and Mandy had seen the nest. James handed his binoculars to Mandy.

"I can't see very clearly," he grumbled, taking off his glasses and rubbing his eyes. "You have a look."

She focused the binoculars, resting them on a boulder to keep them steady. "There's another osprey sitting in the nest. Her mate must have been bringing her food."

"That must mean the eggs are about to hatch," James interrupted excitedly.

"Oh, wow," Mandy whispered, breathlessly. As the male bird flew away from the nest, Mandy followed it, giving James a running commentary. "Yep," she said, speaking softly. "He's smaller than the female. Remember the illustration we saw in Dad's book?"

Mandy was concentrating so hard that she did not hear Hazel come up quietly behind her.

"Mandy," she whispered.

Mandy jumped and the binoculars swung heavily around her neck.

"Hazel!" she said, startled. "You scared me! We didn't know you were here!"

"Sorry." Hazel patted Mandy's shoulder and smiled. "That's the whole idea, really! Isn't he magnificent?" She nodded in the direction of the male osprey. "I've been watching him hunt," she told them. "He's been patrolling the water for hours, looking for fish near the surface. I saw him hover and dive. He practically vanished right under the water to get his dinner!"

Mandy glanced at her watch. "That reminds me — we need to get back for supper."

"Yes," James agreed, adding, "Hazel, did you see the letter from the fishermen in the paper?"

"I did." She frowned. "Isn't it a shame that some people don't appreciate having these gorgeous birds around?"

James called to Blackie, who was sniffing around in the bushes.

"Let us know if we can help out, OK?" Mandy said. "We came up to check that the ospreys were all right after we read the letter in the paper, but you're obviously keeping a good eye on them."

"We're doing our best," said Hazel. "And I'll let you know if anything happens."

As they headed back along the river, Mandy kept her fingers crossed that the only news would be good news about the eggs hatching — and not that the precious ospreys had come to any harm.

Nine

"Slow down, Tucker!" Dr. Adam laughed. The puppy had planted one paw in his food bowl to steady it as he ate.

"He learned that from Domino," Mandy said. "Holding the bowl still, I mean. He used to chase it all over the floor!" She was holding Angel in her lap, sitting on the floor in their kitchen.

"Sleepyhead," Dr. Emily said, smiling as the little puppy turned circles in Mandy's lap before settling down and closing her eyes.

"Uh-oh," said James. "Has anyone seen Patches? She's vanished again."

Mandy looked around the kitchen. Sure enough, their little escape artist was nowhere to be seen.

James began opening kitchen cabinets. "Got you!" he said, pulling open a door that had been ajar.

Patches popped out of the cupboard under the sink with a sponge in her mouth. "I don't think you want to eat that," James warned, trying to remove it. But Patches held on with her tiny teeth and braced her front legs stiffly against the floor to pull against him.

Suddenly, Domino pounced on his sister, trapping Patches's tail under his paw. Patches dropped the sponge at once and turned to launch herself at her brother.

"You can't eat another mouthful," Dr. Adam told Tucker. "You'll pop." He removed the bowl and took it over to the sink, stepping carefully to avoid the tumbling puppies.

"Both the girls are getting visits from potential adopters today," said Dr. Emily. "Mr. Hearn is coming to see Patches, and Elise will be here to spend some time with Angel."

Mandy felt the familiar pang of sadness at the thought of parting with the puppies. She reminded herself again just how important it was to find them the right homes.

"That's great," she said, trying to sound bright. Then she added, "Mom, don't you think Fireman Hartley would make a great dog owner? You know, the fireman at the Walton fire station?"

"Firemen do have a soft spot for Dalmatians," Dr. Adam remarked.

"It's more than that, though," Mandy said. "Fireman Hartley obviously loves dogs, and Walton deserves to have a fabulous pair of Dalmatians at their fire station."

"Well, I guess we don't have anything to lose by asking," Mandy's mom reasoned, adding, "How can he resist? They're an adorable bunch. Patches the adventurer, Domino the live wire . . ."

"Angel the baby," Mandy put it.

"And Tucker the tub!" James finished.

"Poor Tucker," said Dr. Adam. "There's nothing wrong with a healthy appetite!" He patted his own stomach and everyone laughed.

"Can we take the puppies outside?" James asked, scooping up Patches before she could climb into another cupboard.

"Why not? It's a gorgeous day," Dr. Emily said. She turned to Mandy's dad. "You're on fresh newspaper duty in the puppies' room." She grinned. "Get to it!"

Dr. Adam groaned. "There's no peace in this house! Oh, by the way, I offered to drop off some cattle medication at Henderson's farm this afternoon."

"Can James and I come?" Mandy said. "And can we bring Domino and Tucker? The girls will have to stay here because Mr. Hearn and Elise are coming to see them. But the boys would love to have an outing! They're old enough to go outside as long as they don't come in contact with any other dogs."

"I don't see why not," Dr. Adam said. "They've had their first set of vaccinations and you and James should be able to keep an eye on one each."

"Great!" said James. "Leashes?"

"Over there," Mandy told him, just as the phone rang. She sprang for it.

"Hello?"

"Mandy? It's Hazel." She sounded very far away, and Mandy guessed that she was out by the falls. She pictured her on the stool in the blind, looking up at the ospreys' nest.

"Hi, Hazel," she replied. James sat down at the kitchen table to wait. Domino took hold of his sock and shook his head.

"I'm at the blind," Hazel confirmed. "I've got some bad news, I'm afraid. Part of the nest has fallen away. I don't know how it happened."

"What!" cried Mandy. "Are the eggs still there?"

"All safe," Hazel reassured her. "It's just that a clump of bracken and twigs has come loose from the side. I checkcd. The eggs are not in danger of falling out, but still. . . ."

"Oh, the poor parents must be so worried," Mandy said. The line crackled with static, and she held the phone away from her ear for a moment. "Hazel? Are you there?"

"I'm here. I'm out here on my own." There was a pause. "Mandy? I also wanted to tell you that I found a pen-light. It looks like it might be James's."

"You're breaking up," Mandy said. "But thanks for letting us know."

"Look, I'd better go. I'll talk to you soon."

The line went dead. Mandy turned to James. He was on the floor, covered in playful pups, but he lifted his head. "What happened?" he asked.

"The eggs are OK but part of the nest broke and fell," Mandy explained.

"Poor ospreys," James said. "They worked so hard to build that nest."

"Ready?" said Dr. Adam, stepping back into the kitchen.

"I'll take the girls into the yard," Dr. Emily offered. "Come, Patches. Come on, Angel."

"Thanks, Mom." Mandy clipped on Tucker's leash.

Domino sat very still to have his leash put on. He was

already learning his manners, and Mandy hoped he'd be a good example to his brother.

Her dad was obviously thinking along the same lines. "Blackie could learn a thing or two from these puppies," he observed drily, grinning at James.

James sat in the back of the Land Rover with Tucker in his arms. Beside him, Mandy held Domino, but as soon as the doors closed, the two puppies struggled to get free. After a while, Domino got tired of trying to escape and amused himself playing with Tucker's tail and ears instead. When Dr. Adam pulled up at the Henderson's farm, Mandy and James let the puppies wander around the small front yard on their leashes. Domino found a ball, and Tucker rolled on his back on the warm grass.

Suddenly, a large crossbreed dog appeared around the corner of the house, its hackles raised. Mandy scooped up Domino and hurried back to the car, quickly followed by James. There was no point letting the puppies get scared by bigger dogs who wanted to protect their territory.

"That wasn't much of an outing for them," Dr. Adam said when he returned and found them all sitting in the Land Rover.

"No, not really," Mandy admitted. "But we're going to

be driving past the fire station in a minute — why don't we go in and introduce Tucker and Domino to Fireman Hartley?"

"I'll bet he'd love to see the puppies," said James, as Tucker licked his face.

"Right," Mandy's dad said. "We'll go in, but we won't stay long because he'll be working."

"Tucker doesn't like his leash," complained James, as the puppy began scratching at his collar for the umpteenth time.

"He'll get used to it," Dr. Adam said cheerfully. He parked the Land Rover in the fire station parking lot. Mandy got out and put Domino down. He strained ahead happily, wanting to explore this new place. Mandy suddenly felt shy. She hoped that Fireman Hartley was around to see them, and that the puppies would not be an annoyance to the fire station staff.

Tucker and Domino tripped and tumbled along on their leashes as they crossed the car park to the main entrance. Tucker found a discarded Popsicle stick and licked it for the last traces of sugar.

The first person Mandy saw was the red-haired woman she'd seen in the dispatch room. She came to the door, smiling a welcome.

"Hello!" she said. A hair clip that had been pinned to her auburn hair fell to the floor and Domino leaped forward to pick it up. "Oh! How adorable!" she said, kneeling down to pet him. Tucker bustled over to join in, licking anywhere he could reach.

"Hello," Mandy replied, rescuing the hair clip. "I think you'll have to wash this."

"That's OK," she said. "I'm Lynn, by the way. You two came in the other day, didn't you?"

"That's right," said James. "Is Fireman Hartley here, please?"

"Yes, he is. Is he expecting you?"

"Um . . . no," Mandy confessed. "But we won't take more than a minute of his time."

Lynn stood up and poked the hair clip back into her hair. Mandy wondered if she'd forgotten that it had just been licked by a puppy. "Come in — all of you!" she invited. "I'll get Bob for you."

A friendly face appeared in the open door. "Did somebody say my name?"

Mandy smiled. "Hello, Fireman Hartley."

"Mandy and James, hello!" he said. His eyes went to the floor, where two eager little tails were thumping out a greeting. "Are these your little orphans?" he said, kneeling down. Tucker stood up on his hind legs and took Fireman Hartley's finger in his mouth. Domino tried to squeeze between his knees, and James had to tug hard on the leash to discourage him.

"Ouch! Easy there, tiger," Bob Hartley warned Tucker, smiling. Domino grabbed the cuff on the officer's pants and began to tug at it, growling playfully. Fireman Hartley stood up.

Several more staff members had gathered to admire the puppies. Mandy felt very proud of Tucker and Domino. Their coats shone with good health, and they were brimming with trust and good nature. Tucker and Domino lapped up all the attention, rolling onto their backs and wriggling their paws in the air to have their tummies rubbed. When James dropped the leash, Domino ran away as fast as his small legs on slippery linoleum could carry him. Lynn caught up with him as he was heading out of the door.

Mandy turned back to Fireman Hartley. "We thought—" she began, but her explanation was drowned out by the ringing of a shrill alarm bell. Domino and Tucker froze, then darted behind Mandy's legs. Mandy patted their heads to calm them.

The men who had been admiring the puppies started running toward the racks around the engine room.

"Turnout gear!" someone shouted, and Mandy saw a man sliding on a pair of long gloves.

Mandy stood stock-still, unsure what to do. Then Tucker began to bark frantically, and Bob Hartley took a step forward and stepped on Domino's front paw. The puppy howled in astonished protest. Fireman Hartley lost his balance and fell, sprawling face-first onto the floor.

"Are you all right?" Mandy gasped, lunging at Domino and picking him up. James grabbed Tucker and wrapped his arms protectively around the puppy. Around them, the sound of sirens rang out in all directions.

Fireman Hartley got up with as much dignity as he could manage. He turned to Mandy and James. "It's OK. The puppies are just nervous," he said, smoothing his hair back off his forehead.

A man in firefighting gear appeared with a sheet of paper in his hand. "Warehouse blaze on the outskirts of Walton, Bob," he reported.

"OK," said Fireman Hartley. "Let's go!" He started to follow the other fireman toward the engine room.

In Mandy's arms, Domino squirmed to get down. "I'm sorry we got in the way," she apologized.

Bob Hartley paused and looked over his shoulder. "It's not your fault. It's just that a fire station isn't really a good place for puppies." He shut the door behind him, and seconds later two fire engines roared out of the station, sirens wailing.

"That didn't go very well at all." Mandy moaned, putting her chin into her hands. She was sitting at the kitchen table with James and her parents, having lunch. "We didn't even get a chance to suggest that Fireman Hartley give the puppies a home." They were back at Animal Ark and Mandy had not been able to eat a bite so far.

James was eating heartily but he paused to look as disappointed as Mandy felt. "We really blew it." He sighed.

"Don't worry," said Dr. Emily. "We'll find Tucker and Domino a good home — or *two* good homes. And at least Fireman Hartley wasn't hurt."

"It was unfortunate timing, that's all," said Mandy's dad. He stood up to put his plate in the sink. "Looks like rain this afternoon. I'll have to postpone my trip to see the ospreys."

"Well, you can come into the clinic and help me look at Barclay's teeth. That dog is as strong as an ox and it's impossible to open his mouth if he doesn't want you to!"

"I will," Dr. Adam agreed. "But first, I have to find my other shoe —"

Mandy grinned. "Last seen in Patches's mouth, heading up the stairs."

Dr. Adam groaned again and Mandy and James burst out laughing.

As she washed the lunch dishes, Mandy kept glancing through the window at the sky. It had grown ominously dark. A brisk wind was whipping the tops of the trees, spilling delicate new green leaves to the ground.

"I'll bet it's going to hail," James said, rubbing a dish towel over a china plate.

"It's weird to have a storm after all the good weather," Mandy observed. Just then, there was a woosh of wind, and a thin branch cracked and tumbled from a tree outside the kitchen.

"Wow!" said James. "Did you see that?"

Mandy put down the dishcloth and turned to face James. "I'm thinking about the ospreys. Will the nest be safe in this wind, do you think?"

The windowpane rattled as another gust shook the frame.

James shrugged. "I'm not sure," he admitted.

"Well, that nest isn't as strong as we thought. Part of it has already broken off, and the rest could be blown to bits. Hazel might need our help."

Dr. Adam turned the wipers on full speed to cope with the downpour lashing the windshield. "Luckily for us, Barclay was in a cooperative mood, so your mom should be able to manage on her own," he told Mandy. "I hope Hazel is equipped for this fierce rain."

"She can take shelter in the blind," Mandy said. "It looked pretty sturdy." Just then, her father's cell phone rang. Mandy snatched it up from the console between the front seats. "Hello?"

"Is that you, Mandy?" Hazel's voice sounded even fainter than before.

"Yes, it's me. Hi, Hazel." Mandy cupped her hand around the mouthpiece of the phone. She could hardly hear above the noise of the rain and the car tires gouging at the dirt on the road.

"I got this number from your mom. Can you help me?" Hazel sounded breathless. "I'm worried about the osprey nest. I think I'm going to need a hand here and I can't get a hold of Steve or anyone else." Her voice began to break up as the line crackled.

"We're on our way there now," Mandy yelled. "Don't worry, Hazel."

"Oh, thanks," Mandy heard — and the line went fuzzy, then still.

Dr. Adam drove as fast as the weather allowed. He parked the car on the grassy shoulder and they all piled out.

As Mandy slammed her door, a blast of wind and rain caught her straight in the face and she gasped. The wind seemed to blow in circles, coming first from one direction, then the next. The hood of her rain coat billowed and flapped and her hair flew free, until it became soaked and clung to her head.

James hunkered down into the collar of his coat. "Gale force!" he yelled, and Dr. Adam nodded. He leaned into the wind as he led the way across the field, half running in his hurry to reach Hazel and the nest.

Mandy tried to keep her spirits up as she battled along. The wind howled around her ears, making goose bumps prickle her skin. *The ospreys will be safe*, she told herself. *They* must *be safe!* They were so helpless, so fragile. To reach the nest and find the eggs shattered on the ground would be too much to bear!

"Look!" Her dad had stopped. "Isn't that Hazel?" He pointed to a small figure struggling a few yards behind a large sheet of canvas that flapped madly in the wind.

Mandy put up her hand to keep the rain out of her eyes. "The blind!" she said. "It's blowing away!"

The camouflaged dome had ripped free of its pegs and was billowing across the field like a loose sail. Hazel was racing to catch up with it.

"I'll go and help her," shouted Dr. Adam. "You and James go to the nest. Wait for me at the bottom of the tree!"

"Right," Mandy said. "Come on, James."

"I hope she saves the blind!" James yelled, trotting to keep pace with Mandy. Head down, she battled forward. All she could think of was the wind plucking the ospreys' nest from the tree and flinging it to the ground, the precious eggs smashing. . . .

"Come on!" she cried again and began to run up to the crest that led down into the hidden valley.

"Mandy!" James called. "Wait!"

"Come on, James!" she pleaded. She turned back to look at James. He'd stopped running altogether. Mud was spattered up his legs, almost to his knees. The lenses of his glasses were puddled with rain.

"No, wait!" James said again, and Mandy was just starting to feel annoyed when she suddenly understood what James was trying to say. He was pointing down into the valley, breathing hard.

There was a man at the foot of the ospreys' nesting tree!

"It's Steve!" James gasped. "See him? Hazel must have gotten a hold of him after all."

Mandy stared at the man. She saw him stagger, then sit down and lean against the trunk.

"That's not Steve," she told James, clutching on to his arm to support herself as the wind threatened to topple her over. "Steve is thinner and shorter and he's got a beard. . . . That's *not* Steve, James. Come on!" And she ran down the steep grassy slope toward the river.

The man looked up quickly as Mandy pelted toward

him. He was resting his back against the trunk of the
tree with the nest in it. He'd taken off one shoe and
rolled his sock down. He was rubbing his ankle, which
looked swollen and was rapidly turning purple.

"Are you OK?" Mandy panted.

"I think I broke my ankle," he said between gritted
teeth.

Now that she was closer, Mandy recognized him. He

was the fisherman they'd seen on their first visit to the waterfall.

"Have you been fishing today?" she asked in surprise, nodding at the backpack on the ground beside him. Before he could reply, James arrived, dripping and red-cheeked.

"That looks painful," he said, frowning at the man's leg. "Do you need help?"

The man looked around to say something when Mandy spotted a familiar shape making its way down the side of the valley on the other side of the river.

"Dad!" she called. She waved at her father, who raised his arm.

There was a crack of thunder, and Mandy looked up at the nest, then quickly back at the man on the ground. She didn't want to give the nest away just in case he didn't know it was there. When Dr. Adam joined them, hopping nimbly across the rocks in the river, Mandy explained what had happened. When her father was looking directly at her, she pointed discreetly at the nest above them, then put a finger to her lips. Dr. Adam nodded, unnoticed by the fisherman who was lacing up the shoe on his injured foot.

"Where's Hazel?" James asked, flicking water off his forehead.

"Hazel went to get a . . . a friend," Mandy's dad replied,

being careful not to mention the bird-watching team. Mandy guessed that he meant Steve.

"Ouch," said the man, as he tried to stand up.

"I wouldn't try that," Dr. Adam advised. "I'll drive you into town. You need to see a doctor." He put an arm around the man's shoulder, who was white-faced with pain. "See you two later."

"You're staying out in this weather?" the man asked, looking at Mandy with a puzzled expression.

"School project," Mandy said, thinking quickly. "It's on . . ."

". . . on weather," James finished for her.

Dr. Adam coughed loudly to smother a laugh, and there was another crack of thunder. Tiny balls of hail began falling.

"You must be very dedicated students," the man said, as Dr. Adam helped him limp away.

"I'll come back as soon as I can," Mandy's dad promised. "Stay right here, OK?"

Mandy nodded, and waited for the men to get out of earshot before she spoke. She had spotted a cluster of twigs clinging perilously to the forked branches at the top of the tree, and she wanted to share the good news with James. "It's still there!" she said, pointing.

"Thank goodness!" James said. He wrung out the

bottom of his T-shirt, which had escaped from his jeans and was soaked. "Oh, look! That man left a backpack behind."

Mandy studied the canvas bag. "I wonder where his fishing rod is." she said. "He'd never fit it in there."

"Yeah," James said. "Something's not right. I'm going to take a look in the bag."

"James! Should you?" Mandy was concerned that they were about to get into trouble. She looked up. Her father and the man were just specks in the pelting rain, climbing slowly up the far end of the valley.

When Mandy looked back, James was already peering into the fisherman's bag. "Look at this! Binoculars. What do you think he needed these for? Spotting fish?"

"Do you think he could have been spying on the nest?" Mandy asked. She hugged herself. She was shivering now, whether from the chilly rain or growing anxiety, she didn't know.

"Probably not. Hazel would have seen him," James reasoned.

"Maybe not, if he stayed hidden in the trees. Especially if Hazel was taking shelter from the rain in the blind." A stab of cold fear clutched at Mandy's stomach. "Maybe he did something to the nest when she wasn't watching." She went over to the tree. "James! Come and see this."

Several of the lower branches were bent and broken, and the wood inside looked clean and pale as if it had only recently snapped. As rain coursed down the main trunk and dripped steadily from the branches, Mandy started to wonder if the man had hurt his ankle falling out of the ospreys' tree.

"Looks like he tried climbing up," James said, frowning. "I wonder how far he got before he fell?"

"James!" Mandy begged. "I've got to get the harness and climb up. He might have taken the eggs out of the nest!"

There was a gust of wind so strong that James swayed on his feet. Thunder rumbled across the valley. Mandy bit her lip. She couldn't climb the tree without James's help, but would he agree when the weather seemed to be getting even worse?

To her relief, he nodded. "I'll get the equipment," he said. "Wait here."

Mandy sheltered against the trunk of the tree and watched James sprint across the river. He slipped on the second stepping-stone, and his foot crashed into the rushing water, but he hardly hesitated. He ran until he reached the spot where the hide had been, and Mandy saw him bend down to pick up the supplies she needed. She looked up at the nest again and was blinded by rain pelting into her eyes. By the time she looked back, James was already on her side of the river.

"Here," he said, shaking out Steve's climbing harness.

He helped her into the harness, fastening the straps with shivering fingers. Then he made a stirrup out of the palms of his hands. She couldn't climb into the tree as easily as before because the lowest branches were broken.

"Up you go," he encouraged her. "And be careful, please." Under his dripping hair, his brown eyes were very serious. Mandy knew he was concerned for her, but appreciated that he was as eager as she was to protect the ospreys.

She carefully placed her foot in his hand and heaved herself up, and James grunted as she grabbed hold of the nearest, sturdy branch. She saw Steve's rope dangling a few feet above her, swaying in the wind. She reached for it and clipped it to her harness, then wiped her wet hands on her jeans. She knew the rope was firmly attached to the top of the tree, so it would stop her from falling if she slipped off a branch. She was as safe as if Steve were there to hold it himself, but it felt very different to be climbing the tree without him.

"Okay?" James called, shielding his face as he peered up at her.

"Yes," Mandy said. It seemed a long way up but she knew she had to make sure the nest was safe.

Above them, making distinct sounds of alarm, the pair of ospreys began to circle. Mandy hoped they understood that she didn't want to hurt their eggs.

"Do you think they might attack us?" James asked, echoing Mandy's thoughts.

"No," Mandy answered more confidently than she felt. "I'll come down as soon as I've seen the eggs, and hopefully the parents will return to the nest then."

She tried not to look down as she hauled herself from one branch to the next. She concentrated on reaching the nest as quickly and safely as possible, knowing as she climbed that she was the sole cause of the parent birds' distress. At last, she reached the branch that gave her a perfect view right into the nest.

"I made it," she called down to James. "I can see right in . . . and, oh! Oh, *James*!" Mandy's breath caught in her throat and her eyes suddenly stung with hot tears.

"What?" James said from far below. But Mandy didn't answer. "Are you OK?" he prompted.

"Shhhh!" Mandy hissed. The female osprey dived over her head, making a shrill *crik crik* sound. She was frantic to scare Mandy away.

Mandy ducked down until her head was below the level of the nest. She had seen enough. Not two beautiful, pale pink, speckled eggs, but tiny, fluffy — and very damp — heads. Four bewildered beady brown eyes staring up at her, blinking in the rain. Tiny, determined beaks opening and closing, demanding a meal. Beside them, a third egg lay whole and still.

Mandy scrambled down the tree as if she'd been climbing all her life and jumped triumphantly down beside James. "Chicks!" she announced. "Two have hatched. They're just perfect!"

"I'd love to see them," said James, shaking water out of his hair. "But the parent birds are terrified. We should leave them in peace for now."

Mandy saw her father striding toward them along the river, shrouded in a soggy jacket that clung to him like a second skin.

"Everything all right?" he shouted.

"Oh, yes," Mandy yelled back. "Everything is more than all right, Dad! We've got amazing news!"

All the way back to Animal Ark, Mandy and James bombarded Dr. Adam with questions about the fisherman. What had he said he was doing? Was his ankle broken? Had he been trying to get up into the tree to steal the eggs?

"Whoa!" Dr. Adam said, holding up his hand. "I don't know, is the answer. He didn't say anything much. I dropped him off at the Fox and Goose, and he said he would call a doctor from there. That's all I know."

"I bet he'd planned to take the eggs," Mandy said heatedly, glaring at the man's backpack on the floor at her feet. "Oh, Dad! You should have seen those chicks! They're adorable."

"I wish I had," said Dr. Adam. "I'm sure they were," Adam Hope agreed, his voice stern, "but I can't believe you climbed that tree without anyone to help you." He glanced sideways at Mandy. "It was an incredibly dangerous thing to do, and I don't ever want you to think about doing something like that again."

Mandy knew he was right. Even though she'd had James at the bottom of the tree, there would have been nothing he could have done if she'd lost her footing. She remembered what it felt like to cling to the top of the swaying, windswept tree and for a moment she felt sick with nerves. "Okay, Dad," she promised in a small voice.

It was still lashing with rain. Mandy thought longingly of a hot bath and looked across at her father. Drops of rain trickled down the side of his face and sparkled in his beard. "We'll have to toss a coin for who gets the first hot bath," she said.

When Dr. Adam came to a stop outside Animal Ark, Dr. Emily was standing in the doorway. "Are you OK? How are the eggs?" she called.

"Two of them have hatched!" James told her, kicking off his muddy shoes on the doorstep.

"They're beautiful, Mom," Mandy said as she struggled out of her drenched jacket.

"Come in and get dry," urged Dr. Emily. "I want to hear all about it. And I've got four puppies in the kitchen who will be very pleased to see you back!"

The kitchen at Animal Ark was soon festooned with dripping clothing. Dr. Emily made hot chocolate and handed mugs to Mandy and James, who sat on the floor to be close to the puppies. Mandy's father had taken a cup of tea upstairs to sip in a hot bath.

"The chicks are so tiny!" Mandy said. "I can't believe how lucky I was to see them." She moved her mug out of reach of Tucker, whose eager nose was quivering at the scent of hot chocolate. In Mandy's lap, Angel yawned and licked Mandy's wrist with a delicate pink tongue.

"You really think that man was trying to rob the nest?" Dr. Emily asked.

James nodded. "He didn't have a fishing rod with him, and those broken branches were very suspicious." He took a sip from his mug. "Uh-oh." He pointed to the corner of the kitchen.

Domino had unearthed a large, muddy potato from the vegetable basket. He was driving it across the floor with his nose, his tail wagging furiously. Dr. Emily scooped up the potato and gave the puppy a rubber toy instead.

Mandy moved Angel and stood up. "I'm going to call Hazel," she said.

"Good idea," said James, rolling a ball to Patches.

Mandy dialed the cell phone number, and Hazel answered.

"It's Mandy," she said.

"Oh! Mandy," Hazel said. "I'm on my way back to the river. I've got Steve with me. Is everything all right?"

"We're back home now," Mandy told her. "The nest is safe and two of the eggs have hatched! There are two adorable chicks in the nest. We found a man at the foot of the ospreys' tree. He had hurt his ankle. He said he'd been fishing but the lower branches had been damaged and we think he was lying. . . ."

Mandy trailed off, suddenly worried that she'd lost the connection. "Hazel?"

"Yes, I'm here. That's awful. Where is he now?"

"Dad drove him to the Fox and Goose. He said he was going to phone a doctor."

"At least he's nowhere near the nest now. We'll keep a look out for any suspicious-looking fishermen, just in case he or one of his friends comes back. We'll make sure there's a constant watch on the nest until the chicks are able to fly. Then we'll tag the chicks as soon as they are old enough and, hopefully, see them through another breeding cycle. With your help, Falling Foss could have a population of ospreys to be proud of!"

"I hope so," Mandy said.

"Say thank you to James and your dad, for me, OK?" Hazel asked, and Mandy said she would. She replaced the receiver feeling quite proud and a little maternal about the tiny chicks. She was the first human to have seen them! And maybe one day she would see them swoop and dive over the river, feeding chicks of their own.

Dr. Emily had started the next round of puppy feeding, with James's help. "Hazel must be so happy," she said, smiling at Mandy.

"She was," Mandy said. "She and Steve are on their way to the nest now."

"Good," said Dr. Emily, gently moving Tucker back to his own bowl. "Now, I have some exciting news of my own."

"News?" said James. "For us?"

"Bob Hartley has a friend at the Transport Museum in Walton. He wants to take some pictures of the vintage fire engine for a magazine, and Mr. Hartley suggested he use Domino and Tucker as canine models to add an authentic historical touch!"

Mandy jumped in the air with excitement. "That's a great idea!" she cried, making Patches break off from eating and bark.

"And good publicity for the puppies," James added. "A dog-loving reader is bound to want to give them a home."

"I'm sure you're right," Mandy's mom said. "We may not have been lucky with Fireman Hartley, but we're on the road to success now, I'm sure of it."

Ebb and Flo

Ten

The following morning was Sunday. Mandy had set her alarm clock for six. She smothered its ringing before it woke her parents and went quietly downstairs to spend time with the puppies. She had always known she would only be their foster mother for a little while, but it was getting harder and harder to imagine them going to new homes. At least Angel was going to stay in the village, and she'd see Patches whenever Mr. Hearn visited her grandfather.

The puppies were curled up in their basket in a cozy heap, fast asleep. Angel was at the bottom of the pile, lying on her back. Mandy drew the curtain and soft dawn light filtered in. She looked up at the sky, which had that freshly washed look about it. There was no trace of lingering storm clouds. She smiled, picturing the osprey chicks safe in their nest, watched over by Hazel and Steve. She kneeled to drop kisses on the puppies' small, smooth heads and as each pup in turn woke up, their tails began to thump happily. They stretched and yawned, showing their small pink tongues.

"Today is a special day," Mandy told Tucker and Domino seriously. "I hope you're going to behave better than you did last time."

Each puppy regarded her with solemn brown eyes. Then Angel reached up and gave Mandy a thorough face washing, making her laugh. She was so pretty; almost pure white, with only a few scattered spots of black. Patches, ever adventurous, pounced on the hem of Mandy's pajama bottoms and began to tug. Mandy was going to miss them so much!

She turned her attention to the boys, who were wrestling in the basket. Separating them, she tried to get them to sit still to be brushed, but neither of them was interested in being groomed. They continued tumbling around, while Mandy made swipes at their coats with the soft bristled brush.

"Don't you get it?" She laughed. "You're going to have your photograph taken today! You have to look your best."

In the end she gave up and took them into the yard. After they had chased their tails and tumbled across the grass for a while, she called them to her again. "Come on! It's breakfast time. In we go."

Four plump little bodies, a beautiful blur of black-and-white shapes, came tripping over to her on stumpy legs, tails waving, and filed indoors obediently. They really were the most gorgeous puppies!

"Everybody ready?" Dr. Adam asked.

Mandy was cleaning Tucker's mouth with a soft cloth. "Tucker's gotten dirty again. I'll be ready in a second," she said. Just then, the phone rang. She passed the cloth to James and picked the phone up.

"It's me," Hazel said.

"Hello, Hazel," Mandy replied.

"I just wanted to tell you that Steve and I checked the nest today. The chicks are doing well — the mother osprey is feeding them — and the third chick has hatched!"

"Oh!" Mandy said. "I'm so *glad*. Is it all right?"

"Looks fine," she answered. "It's smaller than the others, but moving around well and making a lot of noise!"

"That's such good news," Mandy said. "No sign of the fisherman?"

"None," Hazel told her. "But we've given your description of him to the police, just in case. And we're watching the nest night and day."

"Thanks for letting us know," Mandy said.

"Thank *you*," Hazel said with feeling. "The SPB owes you!"

Dr. Emily drove James, Mandy, and the two puppies into Walton. The sun shone down out of a flawless sky, soaking up the puddles from yesterday's storm, and they were able to see plainly the damage the wind had done to the trees.

Mandy felt sad again, and she could tell James was a bit gloomy, too. They would be saying good-bye to Angel and Patches in just a few days. They were nearly eight weeks old. Mandy reminded herself that parting with the puppies had been their goal in the first place, and she should be feeling happy.

"Cheer up," said Dr. Emily, as she pulled into the parking lot. "We've still got Tucker and Domino to care for, remember?"

"That's true," Mandy said, slipping the leash on Tucker. She put Angel and Patches out of her mind. Today was a big day for the boys.

They trotted happily into the fire station, their noses twitching excitedly. A young fireman in uniform met them in the foyer and introduced himself as Mark Cutter.

"The curator from the Transport Museum is here. He's going to take the photographs," he explained. "He's in the shed with the engines setting up his lights." He bent down to pet the puppies. "Hello, little guys!"

"Where would you like us to wait?" Dr. Emily asked, just as Fireman Hartley appeared in a doorway.

He shook Mandy's mother's hand, glancing down carefully so he didn't step on a tiny paw. Both puppies' tails were wagging hard, and Tucker gave an excited "yip" followed by a playful growl.

"Nice to meet you," Bob Hartley said, shaking Dr. Emily's hand. "We've met before, of course," he added, smiling at Mandy and James. Then he looked down at the carpet, where four bright and curious eyes looked up at him. "We've met, too," he said with a grin. He crouched down and rested his hand on Domino's head. "I nearly flattened you last time," he said. "Sorry about that. You're a handsome dog. And you, too!" Tucker stretched his head forward for his own pat, and Mandy relaxed. Fireman Hartley really did like the pups! "I'm sure you're not going to get into any trouble today, are you?" He looked up and winked at Mandy.

Mandy shook her head. "No trouble at all," she promised.

"I see you've brought your own camera," Bob Hartley observed, pointing to James's Pentax. "Come and see our vintage fire engine out back." He turned to Mark Cutter. "I'll take them outside, OK?"

"Sure thing," said Mark.

Mandy and her mother and James followed Mr. Hartley across the parking lot to the roomy, steel-sided shed that housed the Walton fire station's vintage engine. It was a striking shade of shiny red that had been polished to perfection. Every bit of brass gleamed and the leather upholstery shone so brightly Mandy could see her reflection in it.

"This is a horse-drawn steam engine," Fireman Hartley explained. "It was used in the early part of the nineteenth century, which makes it nearly two hundred years old! The dogs would run alongside it, or just ahead of it, trained to keep pace and stay out of the way of the wheels."

Mandy looked at Tucker and Domino. They were sitting calmly, looking around them with interest. "Dalmatians take well to training," she added, and Bob Hartley nodded.

"You're right," he said. "They're an excellent breed."

Fireman Hartley introduced them to the curator, who

was hovering over the nose of the engine peering at a light meter.

"This is Conrad Webb," he announced and the man looked around, smiled, and raised a hand in greeting.

"Hello! Thanks for bringing in these guys," he said. He jumped down from the wheel and crouched down to pet the puppies. He was a tall, thin man, who reminded Mandy of a heron with his long legs and stooping shoulders. "They're gorgeous! Can you let them off their leashes?" he asked. "I'd like to take some shots of them exploring on their own."

James exchanged glances with Mandy. "Okay," she said, and let Domino go. She wasn't sure how obliging the puppies were going to be. She hoped they didn't rush off and hide.

The pups sniffed at the tires and wandered around, being quite cautious but investigating happily, while Mr.Webb snapped away with an impressive-looking digital camera. Tucker stood up with his front paws against the step that led up to the engine and spotted his blurry reflection in the shiny bodywork. He growled, then wagged his tail, cocking his head comically. On the other side of the shed, Domino had come across somebody's sweater, lying in a heap on a chair. He seized a sleeve and tugged it down to the floor, then made off at top speed with his prize trailing behind him.

Mandy gasped.

"Leave it, it's wonderful!" exclaimed Mr. Webb from behind the camera. "This is great stuff!"

When Mr. Webb was satisfied, and the sweater had been retrieved, Dr. Emily helped Mandy to persuade Tucker to sit beside his brother for a close-up on the seat of the engine. To Mandy's surprise, they sat perfectly still, their ears pricked, looking with curiosity at the camera as it whirred and clicked.

Mr. Webb seemed thrilled. "Much better than I had hoped for," he announced.

"Good," said Mandy, hugging the puppies in turn.

"I've got a couple of scrapbook articles and some photographs about Ebb and Flow to show you," Bob Hartley told them. "You remember, the Dalmatians I told you about last time?"

"Oh, yes!" Mandy said.

"I'll grab them from the office," he said, heading toward the main building.

"I'm not sure if Tucker and Domino will sit quietly for much longer," said Mandy's mom. "They're getting a little antsy."

"Can I take them for you?" Mark Cutter offered. He'd come in to watch the photo shoot. "They probably want a drink. I'll take them to the storeroom next door, OK?"

"Good idea." Dr. Emily smiled. James clipped on Tucker's leash and handed it to Mark Cutter.

"Here's Domino," Mandy said. "Thanks."

"Thanks, Mark," said Fireman Hartley, as Mark led Tucker and Domino away. The puppies looked back at Mandy, both of them hesitating for a moment, but then trotted happily after Mark with their tails held straight up.

Mr. Webb began unplugging the big, hot lights from around the engine. James helped him by coiling up the electric wires while they waited for Fireman Hartley to return with the scrapbooks. He came back quickly and carried the books over to a desk at the back of the shed. He flipped smoothly through a bulky scrapbook that held lots of yellowing scraps of newspaper recording the activities of the Walton fire brigade.

"Ebb and Flow!" Mandy cried, spotting the Dalmatians in a photograph.

"That's right," Bob Hartley confirmed. "Here they are getting a medal from the mayor for their heroic work."

"What handsome dogs!" said Dr. Emily.

The pair sat shoulder to shoulder, looking as though they were smiling with pride. Ribbons with small disks had been hung around their necks.

"An award in honor of courage . . ." James began to read.

"Just a minute," Mandy said, holding up her hand to shush him. She had heard a tiny whimpering sound, distant but distinct. When James stopped reading, she strained her ears and heard scratching, a scraping noise, and more whimpering.

"That's Domino and Tucker," she said, looking apologetically at Fireman Hartley. She couldn't believe they were misbehaving now, when things had gone so well during the photo shoot!

"They'll settle down, sweetie," her mom said. "I'm sure they feel confused about being in a strange place, that's all."

But the puppies seemed really unhappy. Their protests grew louder, and Mandy found it hard to concentrate on any of the photographs in the scrapbook.

Mr. Webb appeared, carrying a heavy bag of equipment. "I'll just take this out to my car."

"OK, thanks," said Fireman Hartley.

Domino and Tucker's whimpering had turned to high-pitched, yapping and, seconds later, Mandy heard one long anguished howl. She felt her stomach turn over. That wasn't just the sound of bored puppies. Something was wrong!

Fireman Hartley frowned. "What's bothering them?"

"I'll go and see," Mandy said and shot across the floor toward the door. James was right on her heels.

Mandy had barely gone three strides when an ear-splitting shriek made her stop dead and clap her hands over her ears. Was the fire engine being summoned again?

"Fire!" someone shouted from the main building, and Mandy realized it was the fire station's own alarm. If there was a fire on the premises she had to get to Domino and Tucker right away! She dropped her hands and sprinted the last few steps to the door.

There was a small, windowless one-story room attached to the side of the shed. Mandy guessed this was the storeroom. She opened the door — and both puppies nearly knocked her flat in their haste to get out.

"Domino! Tucker!" Mandy gasped, stumbling backward.

James peered into the room over Mandy's shoulder. "I think we just discovered the fire!" he said. "I smell smoke!"

Mandy pushed the puppies clear of the room and, flinging the door wide, poked her head back in to look around. Flames were curling up the door to a large cupboard in the corner. As Mandy stood there, her mouth wide open in alarm, she saw the white paint start to pop and peel in the heat.

"The fire's in here!" she yelled, finding her voice. "Fire!"

James grabbed Tucker, and Mandy turned to reach for Domino, who was swirling anxiously around her feet. Mandy lifted him quickly into her arms, coughing.

"Fire!" she shouted again, just as Mark Cutter and Bob Hartley burst out of the shed, wielding portable fire extinguishers. Mandy jumped aside to let the men blast a stream of foam into the storeroom. Tucker barked and squirmed in James's arms. Meanwhile, the fire alarm continued to wail, almost loud enough to drown the yelps of the puppies.

Dr. Emily put an arm around James's shoulder and drew Mandy away with her other hand. When they were a safe distance from the fire, she took Domino out of Mandy's arms. He was busily wiping his face with his front paw.

Dr. Emily held him close and examined his eyes. "He's OK. I imagine his eyes are just stinging from the smoke," she decided. "Nobody else hurt?"

"We're fine," Mandy gasped, out of breath with shock. "Is Domino really okay?"

"He's absolutely fine," Mandy's mom confirmed. She had a look at Tucker, who wagged his tail, then coughed. "A little smoke get up your nose?" Dr. Emily asked him, stroking his back. Tucker sneezed.

"It looks like they've put the fire out," said James, pointing to clouds of white smoke billowing from the storeroom. At that moment, the fire alarm stopped dead. The silence made Mandy's ears ring and she shook her head to get her normal hearing back. She and James went closer and peered through the open door.

Bob Hartley was using a small ax to break into the locked cupboard. The lock of the cupboard had melted, and the key was just a molten blob. There were little piles of foam everywhere, but all the flames had been put out. When the wood splintered and gave way, Fireman Hartley used a flashlight to look around the charred inside of the cupboard.

"Looks like a faulty electrical wire," he said. "See, Mark? It must have shorted out and set fire to the wood."

Mandy went back to the shed, where her mother was holding Tucker and Domino. She sat down cross-legged on the floor beside them. Tucker put his nose on her knee and looked up at her with loving eyes.

"Good job," Mandy said, petting them. "You raised the alarm quicker than the real fire alarm! The whole shed could have gone up in flames if it hadn't been for you two." Domino put his front paws on Mandy's chest and licked the tip of her nose.

James agreed. "It was an electrical short in a cupboard," he explained to Dr. Emily. He sat down and Domino promptly climbed onto his lap.

"Everyone all right?" asked Fireman Hartley,

appearing in the doorway. He had foam on his shoes and still carried the ax.

Tucker and Domino wagged their tails.

"We're all fine," Dr. Emily said, adding, "thank you," as Fireman Cutter followed him in with a bowl of water for the thirsty puppies.

Bobby Hartley's face was still flushed with heat from the fire and there was a sooty smear on his cheek. Mandy figured that if there was going to be a fire anywhere, it was probably good to happen in a fire station where everyone knew what to do to put it out.

Domino bounded off James's lap and ran over to Fireman Hartley, looking up at him with his head cocked to one side. Tucker joined his brother, his tail thumping hard against Bob Hartley's legs.

"And you . . ." he said, bending down to cover their silky heads with the palms of his hands, ". . . are clever puppies! You made a commotion for a very good reason."

Both puppies stared at him solemnly. Mandy caught James's eye and smiled. She was so proud of Tucker and Domino. They were so young, yet had reacted instinctively to danger. Was there any chance they could make Mr. Hartley change his mind about having puppies at the fire station?

"We're still looking for a home for Tucker and

Domino," James said, as though he had read Mandy's thoughts.

"Yes, you said . . ." Fireman Hartley raised his eyebrows.

"It looks like fire stations still need Dalmatians, after all?" Mandy put in with a grin.

Bob Hartley looked from one face to another, then back to the two puppies at his feet. Their tails hadn't stopped wagging. Then, to Mandy's dismay, he shook his head. "They did wonderfully today, but a modern fire station is still no place for a pair of young pups. There's no way they could run alongside the engines, that's for sure!"

Mandy guessed he was trying to make a joke so she didn't feel so bad that he was turning the puppies down again. But she didn't feel like laughing. She reached out and let Tucker sniff her hand, leaving a trace of soot behind from his grubby muzzle.

"But they don't have to live here all the time," Mr. Hartley went on. Mandy looked up at him, surprised. He grinned. "I've been thinking about getting a dog," he said. "My daughter is dog crazy and my son would love it. And I dare say Domino and Tucker would soon pick up a few house rules if they came to work with me once or twice a week."

Fireman Cutter nodded. "We'd be happy to help with exercising the pups, Bob. We could clear out a storeroom and make it safe for them to stay in when everyone's out on call."

Mandy felt her heart lurch with hope. She could tell that Fireman Hartley had lost his heart to Domino and Tucker. She couldn't see his face because he was bent down, still stroking the puppies.

"Paw?" he said, holding out his hand. Tucker picked up one small foot, wobbled a bit, and placed a front paw gently in the palm of his hand.

Mandy gasped. "That's just like Dapple!"

"Who?" said Bob Hartley.

"The puppies' mother," Mandy said, her eyes pricking with tears. "We found her in my grandfather's garden, lying in a bed of daisies, just as she was about to give birth." Mandy swallowed and looked at her feet. "Dapple died right after the birth," she finished quietly. "That's why we are so desperate to find good homes for our puppies. It feels like the last thing we can do for Dapple."

"You're right. They deserve the best homes of all after a start like that," Bob Hartley agreed. "I bet they'll need another set of vaccinations and I'll need instructions about feeding. . . ."

Mandy stared at him in astonishment. "You mean you're really going to take them?" She gasped.

Fireman Hartley nodded, his eyes twinkling. "As you say, they've proven that the Walton fire station needs a Dalmatian — or two — around the place. Not to mention the fact that my son and daughter will love them!"

"That's awesome!" Mandy said.

"They can't be adopted for another week yet," Mandy's mom reminded Fireman Hartley. "Why don't you bring your children to the clinic to meet Tucker and Domino, and I'll give you all the information you need then?"

Fireman Hartley nodded. "That's sounds like a very good idea."

Tucker rolled over, as though he understood the good news, and Bob Hartley rubbed his smooth pink tummy.

"Would anyone be interested in having a picture taken outside?" asked Mr. Webb, who had finished straightening up the shed.

"Definitely," Fireman Hartley replied. "I want a picture taken with my new puppies. Come on, boys!"

The puppies scrambled happily after him as he made for the door.

Mandy turned and gave her mother a hug. "They belong here," she said. "It just feels right, somehow."

"Wow!" James said, his eyes round behind his glasses. "We did it. We found homes for all of Dapple's puppies."

"More important," Dr. Emily said, "you found the *right* homes."

Just before they followed Mr. Webb and Fireman Hartley out to the yard, Mandy went over to the scrapbook to take another look at a photograph of Ebb and Flow. They were sitting at the foot of some steps, wearing their Walton fire jackets, with their smooth, spotty heads pressed together, looking alert and dignified.

"At last," she said to James, "Walton fire station has another gorgeous pair of Dalmatians to be proud of!"

"It's not just the fire station that can be proud," James said, his brown eyes sparkling behind his glasses. "Wherever Dapple is, I bet she's watching them right now and feeling even prouder than anyone else!"

ABOUT THE AUTHOR

Ben Baglio was born in New York, and grew up in a small town in southern New Jersey. He was the only boy in a family with three sisters.

Ben spent a lot of his childhood reading. English was always his favorite subject, and after graduating from high school, he went on to study English Literature at the University of Pennsylvania. During his coursework, he was able to spend a year in Edinburgh, Scotland.

After graduation, Ben worked as a children's book editor in New York City. He also wrote his first book, which was about the Olympics in ancient Greece. Five years later, he took a job at a publishing house in England.

Ben is the author of the Dolphin Diaries series, and is perhaps most well known for the Animal Ark and Animal Ark Hauntings series. These books were originally published in England (under the pseudonym Lucy Daniels), and have since gone on to be published in the U. S., and translated into 15 languages.

Aside from writing, Ben enjoys scuba diving and swimming, music and movies. He has a beagle named Bob, who is by his side whenever he writes.